"You've just had a baby. You need care. The baby needs care!" Steve said forcefully.

"I am perfectly capable of taking care of my baby," Jennifer countered. "Besides, we're not your responsibility."

"Look, Ms. Lewis," he began, "I helped bring that little girl into the world, and you even named her after me. Those two details give me some rights about her welfare, and I'm exercising those rights right now. You absolutely cannot be on your own with a newborn."

"Neither you nor anybody else has the right to tell me what's best for me or for Stephanie. Just go."

"I'm sorry," he said quietly. All he knew for sure was that there would be a daddy for little Stephanie. No matter how hard her mommy tried to kick him out of their lives, something told him she really didn't want him to leave.

Dear Reader,

June is a terrific month. It's the time of year when the thoughts of women—and men—turn to love...*and* marriage. Not only does June mark the beginning of those hot, lazy days of summer, it's also a month with a fantastic, fiery lineup from Silhouette Desire.

First, don't miss the sizzling, sensational *Man of the Month, The Goodbye Child* by Ann Major, which is the latest in her popular Children of Destiny series. Also in June, look for *The Best Is Yet To Come,* another story of blazing passion and timeless romance from the talented pen of Diana Palmer.

Rounding out June are four other red-hot stories that are sure to kindle your emotions written by favorite authors Carole Buck, Janet Bieber and—making their Silhouette Desire debuts—Andrea Edwards and Amanda Stevens.

So get out those fans and cool down...then heat up with stories of sensuous, emotional love—only from Silhouette Desire!

All the best,

Lucia Macro
Senior Editor

JANET
BIEBER

THE FAMILY PLAN

SILHOUETTE *Desire*®

Published by Silhouette Books New York

America's Publisher of Contemporary Romance

SILHOUETTE BOOKS
300 East 42nd St., New York, N.Y. 10017

THE FAMILY PLAN

ISBN: 0-373-05646-X

First Silhouette Books printing June 1991

All the characters in this book are fictitious. Any resemblance to actual persons, living or dead, is purely coincidental.

Printed in the U.S.A.

Books by Janet Bieber

Silhouette Desire

Seeing Is Believing #533
The Family Plan #646

JANET BIEBER

admits to being a lifelong romantic and dreamer. However, she hadn't even thought of writing all those dreams until she met a fellow romance addict. Fate took a hand, and a friendship and the writing collaboration of Janet Joyce was born of that meeting. Since that day, she has authored or co-authored over twenty contemporary and historical novels.

Her husband swept her off her feet over twenty years ago, proving that white knights do exist in the twentieth century. They live in Columbus, Ohio, with their son and two daughters, an aging gentle setter and a young, feisty cat. Janet says that when the chaos of three teenagers gets too much, she and the pets escape to her study, where the dog sleeps, Janet spins her dreams out via a word processor, and the cat attacks the paper coming out of the printer.

To my family, especially Brad,
for his help and inspiration

One

———

"The court calls Dr. Steven Barthelmaus to the stand."

Thankful for the excuse to stand up, Jennifer Lewis, attorney for the plaintiff, got on her feet while the expert witness she'd called was sworn in. A dull ache had begun in her lower back not long after the judge had called the hearing to order. As the morning had progressed, the straight-backed chair provided by the court had steadily become an instrument of torture. Upright, Jennifer felt considerably better.

Glancing at her notes one last time, she brushed her hand absently across her swollen abdomen, not surprised to feel a tightening beneath her touch. She'd been having these painless and apparently meaningless contractions for weeks. Braxton-Hicks contractions her doctor had called them. False labor and nothing to worry about.

At her appointment the previous week, he had assured her that despite her increased discomfort, delivery was still at least a month and a half away. "You'll know when it's real labor," he'd promised her.

This wasn't real labor, Jennifer told herself. She'd be far more uncomfortable if it was, wouldn't she?

Glad that this was to be the last testimony before the noon recess, Jennifer prepared to approach the stand. After just two steps, she felt another twinge in her lower back. She tried to ignore it, but this time it didn't just stay in her back nor did it remain a mere twinge.

Pain, sharp and intense, radiated toward her belly and girdled her body with stunning force. In reaction she gripped the edge of the table and bit her lip to keep from crying out.

"Are you all right, Ms. Lewis?" the judge asked.

As quickly as it had struck, the cramp ebbed to nothing and Jennifer was able to let go of the table. "I...I'm fine, your honor," she said, though she wasn't sure she hadn't just perjured herself. She was definitely not feeling fine. Still she saw no reason to request a recess.

The sooner Barthelmaus gave his testimony, the sooner an equitable property settlement could be reached in Nelson versus Nelson. The case had dragged out far longer than anyone had foreseen at the onset and Jennifer was heartily looking forward to its end. What had started out as an amicable dissolution had escalated into a small war, when the matter of the five horses the couple owned jointly had come up. Out-of-court negotiations had broken down. Emotional battle lines had suddenly been drawn not unlike those usually heard in child custody disputes, and the case had been brought before a judge.

Steven Barthelmaus, D.V.M., was the last in a long string of witnesses called by both parties to help settle the dispute over estimated value and "custody" of the horses. Jennifer had her fingers crossed that Barthelmaus's testimony would afford the judge enough information to come to a decision later this very day.

"Dr. Barthelmaus," Jennifer began, "you are a veterinarian?"

"I am."

Normally Jennifer paused and took a good long assessing look at a witness before proceeding with further questions. But today she felt uncharacteristically nervous and fidgety and chose to pace back and forth as she initiated the standard querying. "You are familiar with the five Standardbred horses at Nelson Farm?"

"I am."

He'd emitted only two short words again, the very same ones as before. They were even the ones she'd fully expected him to answer, and hence she'd paid little attention the first time he'd pronounced them. However, this second time the sound of his voice captured her full attention. Something about his tone made her feel less nervous. Jennifer stopped pacing and gave Barthelmaus the customary visual once-over.

She could study the man for a long moment without danger of being accused of gawking. After all, it was standard procedure to size up a witness before beginning questioning. Even a supposedly unbiased expert witness should be assessed for any signs of hostility.

Barthelmaus didn't look hostile. He looked... pleasant, the epitome of the kindly country vet. His features, like his voice, were those one might expect of the stereotypical kindly country vet. However, he wasn't exactly what you'd see in a Norman Rockwell rendition. The man was much too young and dressed too fashionably and expensively.

Instead of the rumpled and leather-elbowed corduroy jacket and plaid flannel shirt Rockwell might have put on his model, Barthelmaus wore a crisp white shirt and a subtly patterned tie that complemented the light blue threads woven through the darker hue of his suit jacket. Expensive fabric expensively tailored, Jennifer judged, since the garment skimmed the man's broad shoulders perfectly. This was no ordinary country vet. But then her client had said Barthelmaus was a renowned equine expert.

Jennifer had done some checking. Both the Ohio Veterinary Medical Association and The Ohio State University College of Veterinary Medicine had substantiated Sue Nelson's estimation of Barthelmaus's expertise, professionalism and ethics. His was a remarkable reputation considering his relative youth.

He was in his early to maybe mid-thirties, she estimated. Blond-haired, ruddy-complexioned and square-jawed. He was no Robert Redford, but pleasant wasn't a strong enough adjective. Good-looking bordering on, yet not quite falling into, the handsome category. But that classification was only if his eyes weren't taken into consideration.

They were the most marvelous blue eyes she'd ever seen, and they instantly catapulted Steven Barthelmaus into serious contention with Redford. Warm and gentle, they matched his voice. They conveyed honesty and trustworthiness and were the most disconcerting pair of eyes she'd ever stared into....

Jennifer caught the sigh before it escaped. Blinking, she took a step back to put more space between herself and Barthelmaus. "When were your services first requested by anyone at Nelson Farm?"

"About six years ago Sue Nelson called me to look over a horse she and Doug had just bought," Barthelmaus answered in the same smooth and easy tones he'd used before. Jennifer heard and felt each syllable settle around her like a warm blanket so comforting she would have liked to snuggle down into its imaginary security and forget all about the pressing business at hand.

Almost hoping for another twinge of pain to take her mind off Barthelmaus's voice and eyes, Jennifer rubbed at the small of her back. "Do you recall the name of that horse?"

"Yes, his name is First Choice. He's a Standardbred gelding who's been a respectable contender in the harness-racing circuit for close to ten years," Barthelmaus supplied. Jennifer had trouble concentrating on the information, let alone trying to remember her next question.

Lord! Did all veterinarians talk this way? Maybe it was an acquired skill designed to soothe nervous animals. If so, this man had it down so pat he probably didn't have to use painkillers on his patients. Just the sound of his voice combined with his warm steady gaze was bound to make them feel better. He probably lulled them into a state of complete relaxation the minute he said hello. She was beginning to feel utterly hypnotized herself.

As much to instigate further speech from the man as to gain the necessary information, Jennifer launched into a series of questions regarding the age and medical history of the horse called First Choice. As Barthelmaus supplied the answers, the sharp ache that had begun again disappeared once more. Even better, she felt more like herself than she had all morning.

"Thank you, Dr. Barthelmaus," she said after he'd finished and felt immediately foolish when she realized her gratitude had been expressed almost gushingly. Her courteous statement had had nothing at all to do with his testimony. She was nowhere near done with her line of questioning. She'd just thanked the man for relieving her discomfort!

Ridiculous! It was purely coincidence that her back ache had totally disappeared while he'd been talking. Jennifer's mind raced to find a way to cover her mistake.

A quick glance at the judge confirmed that he was surprised she'd apparently finished. Before he could turn Barthelmaus over to the opposition, Jennifer quickly came up with a cover. "That was a very thorough description of the horse's medical problems, Dr. Barthelmaus," she stated with a smile.

She took a few steps away from the witness stand and turned toward the courtroom just slightly. "Now, given this animal's age and his history of muscle and tendon damage, is it your recommendation that he no longer be raced?"

"I've recommended that First Choice be rested for several months and then reappraised. The Standardbred is a very sturdy breed of horse and there are cases of horses with worse damage than First Choice going on to win a lot of races after a recuperative period."

Surprise sent Jennifer turning back quickly to face him. Sue Nelson had stated emphatically over and over that First Choice should be retired immediately and permanently from the track and was therefore of far less value than her husband was claiming.

"But isn't it true that fifteen is the absolute maximum age—" she began but the rest of her question dissolved into a long drawn out "Ooooh!"

A cramp, sharper and stronger than any she'd experienced, grabbed at her. She groped for the railing around the stand.

"Ms. Lewis...?" Barthelmaus started to rise but she waved him back into his chair.

Steve followed her directive but unwillingly. He might be an animal doctor, but labor in mammals was pretty much the same whether the expectant mother was a dog, a horse, or a human. He was positive the woman with a white-knuckled grip on the railing beside him was in labor and not just the first stage.

Sue and Doug Nelson could squabble over who got which horse another time. Something far more important than his professional opinion of the overall health of those damned animals and their estimated value was at stake here. As far as he was concerned, a delay wasn't going to make one whit of difference in the settlement.

On the other hand, a baby's debut into the world, human or otherwise, wasn't something that could be postponed until a more convenient time. No matter what the species, the young came when they were ready and it was becoming more and more obvious that little Miss or Mr. Lewis was definitely ready.

"Is it your opinion, Dr. Barthelmaus that—" Another cramp shot around Jennifer's body and she grabbed at the railing again.

"It's my opinion that you should request a recess." Steve purposefully kept his voice low and calm as he rose from the witness chair.

"Please, Dr. Barthelmaus," Jennifer got out between gasps. Her words, meant to make him sit back down, came out sounding like a plea for help. To her utter embarrassment she felt warm liquid gush from between her legs.

Her water had broken. This was the real thing. "Oh . . . no!"

Already on his feet, Steve was beside her before she had a chance to look at the puddle at her feet. "Your honor . . . ?"

Not waiting for permission or any sort of answer, Steve scooped the attorney for the plaintiff up in his arms and started toward the closest exit door, the one directly behind the bench. The white-haired man behind the bench wasted no time in formally declaring the morning's proceedings in recess until further notice.

"Who's your doctor, Ms. Lewis?" Steve asked as he strode through the judge's secretary's office on his way to what he hoped was the man's chambers and a couch.

"William Canfield. Oh, this can't be happening yet. It's way too soon."

"It is happening and somebody thinks the time's just right." He smiled down at her as he shouldered the next door open. To the judge's secretary, he ordered, "Look up Dr. William Canfield's number and tell him—what's your first name?"

"Jen...Jennifer."

"Tell him Jennifer Lewis's water just broke. Tell him where she is and that we'll do the best we can to get her to the hospital in time," Steve called over his shoulder. "Then call an emergency squad to get over here pronto. We've got a lady here who could very well deliver any minute. And when you get finished with all those calls, get in here."

"Just who do you think you are?" Jennifer demanded angrily as he lowered her onto the couch that occupied one wall of the judge's chambers.

"Your rescuer." He tucked a throw pillow under her knees and started slipping her shoes off. "With any luck, the medics will arrive in just a few minutes, but for now you're stuck with me. Any objections?"

Jennifer thought she ought to object. She didn't need rescuing. She could handle anything all by herself...well maybe not everything. After all, if it hadn't been for Barthelmaus's quick actions, she might still be standing in the middle of the courtroom. And he certainly did seem to know what to do.

But still, the man was a horse doctor for God's sakes! A horse doctor with a voice that calmed and comforted and eyes she wanted to lose herself in. If he left the room she might very well start screaming. "No objections, Dr. Barthelmaus."

"The squad is on its way, her doctor's been called, and the judge is running around the building, more or less hysterical, trying to find a doctor or nurse." The attractive brunette who kept Judge Williams's office running efficiently came into the room carrying two snowy white pillows and a stack of sheets so fresh from the laundry they were still encased in protective cellophane. "Anyone else you want called, Ms. Lewis?"

Both Barthelmaus and the woman looked at Jennifer expectantly. "No one except my office, thanks," she said, wishing for the first time since her pregnancy had been confirmed that there was somebody to call, somebody who would be there to hold her hand and rejoice with her when the baby arrived. But there wasn't and she'd known there wouldn't be from the moment she'd decided to have a baby.

It took only a second's glance to see that her rescuer was puzzled by her response. Not so the judge's secretary, at least not that Jennifer could discern. Without so much as a blink of an eye, the woman stepped forward. Introducing herself as Gale Griffith, she stacked the linens on the judge's desk. "Well, then," she began with a cheery smile. "Since I went ahead and called your office, it sounds like we've got everything pretty well covered for the time being."

Patting the crisp white sheets, she explained, "I keep these around for those times the judge ends up sleeping here waiting for a jury to make up its mind. Thought they might come in handy. If push comes to shove, I think I can be of some help. It's been a few years, but I've been through this a couple of times myself. Let's see what we can do to get you a little more ready, just in case this baby's in a real hurry to get here."

Bemused, Jennifer lay on the couch and listened to Gale Griffith take over. This time it was her rescuer being given orders as he was smoothly ushered into the adjoining lavatory and instructed not to return until he was called. With an economy of motion that would have more easily been credited to a delivery room nurse, Gale opened one of the sheets and draped it over Jennifer, stripped the soggy garments from her lower body and slipped another sheet beneath her. "There," she said with a warm smile when she was finished. "Feel better?"

Jennifer started to nod, but another contraction hit. Tears formed at the corners of her eyes as much from fear as from pain. "This isn't real labor. It's too soon, too soon," she chanted nonsensically.

What she was experiencing was real labor, and instinct warned her that the birth was near. Striving for calmness, she tried to remember everything she'd learned about breathing during labor. As she fixated on the large landscape painting hanging on the opposite wall, she thought she heard Gale call someone's name.

Attempting mind over matter, Jennifer tried to lose herself in the forest depicted in the painting. Relax into the peace of the woods she told herself. Walk through the cool shade, listen for birds, spot a squirrel leaping from branch to branch. For a few seconds she was in that place, but the force of what was happening within her body broke her concentration.

Gasping, she squeezed her eyes shut to close out the pain and reached out blindly for something solid to grip. Her hands closed over warm flesh and bone. Someone's hand. Too large to be Gale's. Barthelmaus . . . ?

"Easy, easy girl. Everything's going to be okay," Steve crooned as he knelt beside her. Automatically he slipped into the same manner and tone he used with a young mare or heifer in the same condition as the woman writhing on the couch.

"You're doing fine, girl," he said, keeping up a steady stream of reassurances. Spreading his free hand over her linen-draped belly, he felt the contraction and began a gentle circular massage to ease it.

If speech had been possible between her short breaths, Jennifer would have told him how comforting his touch was. She wasn't used to being stroked so intimately by anyone. But surprisingly, right then this man's touch, virtual stranger that he was, was so welcome she wasn't sure she could last without it. And if earlier she'd only joked to herself that his voice was soothing, she wasn't kidding about it now. She didn't want him to stop talking, even if he was calling her girl as if she were some big old cow.

"Everything is going to be all right," he stated with a smile as he felt her abdomen relax. "Is this your first baby?"

Jennifer nodded as the pain ebbed.

"Then it'll probably be a while yet," he said to ease some of the worry from Jennifer's face. In reality he doubted it would be very long at all. "Try to resist bearing down if you can."

"I'll try...but I can't seem to control anything that's happening right now."

"The forces of nature," Steve said with a teasing grin, though he was feeling far from jovial. *Where was that emergency squad?*

Relaxing now that the pain was completely gone, Jennifer eased her fingers from around Steve's hand. Seeing the deep, red imprints of her nails where she'd dug into his flesh at the apex of the contraction, she gasped. "Oh, I'm so sorry. I've hurt you. I didn't realize—"

"Forget it." Previously unaware of any damage, Steve studied the marks, then smiled. "Nothing to worry about. Usually, I get kicked or bitten."

His smile was infectious and Jennifer returned it. "Your patients don't sound very grateful for your help."

She was pretty when she smiled, Steve thought. Very pretty. Her mouth was soft and wide when her lips weren't pressed tightly together against pain. Her face was a nice oval, though her chin was maybe a little too pointed for him to call the overall conformation a perfect oval.

Her hair, now loosened from the tidy coil she'd worn in the courtroom, framed her features in a blend of gold and brown. Not a brunette, but not quite a blonde, either. Whatever the classification was he liked it and couldn't resist brushing back some wayward wisps for no other reason than to touch her hair and find out if it was as silky as it looked. It was, and he was hard put to keep from burying his fingers in the thick mass.

Why wasn't there a husband or lover to be called? Had some jerk deserted her because she got pregnant or had she recently become a widow? What about family? Surely she had some somewhere. Whatever had happened, she was alone at a time a woman should least be alone and he began to feel the same protectiveness he always felt when confronted with an abandoned animal. Somebody needed to step in and take care of her—at least until she could take care of herself again.

"The patients who bite or kick me are just scared." He tucked her slender hand back into his much larger palm. "How about you? Are you scared?" he asked, but her eyes were already giving him the answer. They were large pools of deep gray that conveyed more than the stress of childbirth. There was a vulnerability in their depths and something else he couldn't quite put into words. She'd been hurt, emotionally, and not just once.

They reminded him of the look in Hugger's eyes when he'd found the half-starved cat shivering under his porch, cold, wet and so weak she'd put up only token resistance to her rescuer. That the animal had been abandoned was obvious, just as obvious as the signs of physical abuse he'd discovered once he'd gotten her cleaned up.

This woman didn't have any physical scars or bruises as far as he could tell, but he'd bet almost everything he owned that she suffered no less severely emotionally than Hugger had physically. There was a touch of the same wariness and distrust in Jennifer Lewis's manner that Hugger had displayed.

"Nothing to be too scared about. Old Doc Barthelmaus is here," he teased. "I promise to see you through this."

The words were out before he realized how true they were. He hadn't been timing Jennifer's contractions, but they were coming close enough together that he knew the birth was imminent. Unless the medics arrived in the next few seconds, he was going to have to deliver this baby.

Briefly he considered taking the coward's way out and making a dash for the door. He'd helped deliver dozens of puppies and a good number of foals, calves and lambs but this human baby would be his first. As quickly as the idea of retreat had formed it disappeared. He was no more likely to abandon Jennifer

Lewis in the midst of delivering her baby on a leather couch in a judge's chambers than he would have left old Hugger out under the porch that stormy night eight years ago.

"But you're a vet, a horse expert and I'm a wo—oh! Oh my!"

"You're a very pretty woman who's about to have a baby. And unless the cavalry arrives in the next few seconds, I'm the only doctor you've got. Trust me?"

His eyes were still conveying the warmth, gentleness and honesty she'd seen in the courtroom. A lifetime of disappointments made it difficult for Jennifer to give her trust. Difficult until Steven Barthelmaus asked. Her nod of agreement came easily.

She tried to return the smile he sent her, but another contraction was girdling her belly and all she could do was dig her nails into Steve's hand once again. "Your poor hand."

"Don't worry about my hand." He grinned, showing hints of dimples in his cheeks and a mischievous light in his eyes. "You can even bite it if you feel the need. My tetanus shot's up to date. How about your rabies shots?"

Despite her pain, Jennifer laughed.

The following minutes would forever be a blur for Jennifer. The powers of nature they'd joked about earlier took over completely and if she'd felt helpless before, the feeling was a hundredfold now. All that was real was the solidity of the hand she gripped with all her might and the warm blue eyes holding her gaze, promising to see her through the ordeal. At some point Steve's strong hand slipped from her grip to be replaced by Gale's softer, far smaller ones.

"Don't leave me," Jennifer cried frantically, not even knowing she'd uttered the words.

As if he were way off in the distance, she heard his voice. "I'm still here. I never break my promises. Trust me, Jennifer."

Trust me were the last words Jennifer made any sense of before the most overpowering need to push down came over her. The words echoed over and over inside her head as nature completely took control. She heard a loud moan of protest, barely realizing the voice was her own. And then a new sound broke through the judge's small chamber.

A newborn baby's lusty wail.

"You have a beautiful little girl," Steve announced as he lifted the baby onto Jennifer's stomach.

"She's perfect," Gale added. "She's just beautiful! Do you know what you're going to call her?"

Jennifer hesitated for a moment then blurted, "Stephanie Gale." She stroked her daughter's tiny damp head, awed by its perfection and the surge of love she felt for this miniature human. Then she looked up to the stunned faces over her and realized what she'd just named her baby. "If it's all right with both of you, that is."

"All right?" Steve hooted with a big grin. "It's more than all right!"

Gale's response was the same. She clapped Steve on the back. "We made a good team, Doc. But, if it's all the same to you, I'd like to retire on our laurels."

Sounds of activity and other voices came from the anteroom beyond the door, and Steve laughed derisively. "Better late than never. The cavalry has arrived, I believe."

It was indeed the emergency squad, and within a few minutes Jennifer and her baby, tucked safely within the circle of her arm, were transferred onto a stretcher. They were being wheeled out of the chamber when Jennifer called for a stop. "Steve . . . ?"

"Right here." He bent over her. Smiling, he caught up her free hand in his and gave it a gentle squeeze.

Now that he was beside her again, Jennifer was at a loss as to why she'd called out for him. It had just seemed so imperative that she see him again, say something, before she was taken away. "Eh . . . thank you," she said, feeling immediately that the words were inadequate for what he'd done for her. "I don't know what would have happened if you hadn't been here."

"You would've been just fine. You did all the work. I just helped out a little."

"But . . . I . . ." Embarrassed to admit openly how important his voice and touch had been during her labor, she pulled herself up short. She'd needed a fantasy during those frightening moments when she'd felt so out of control, but the emergency was over. She didn't need it now and she didn't really need Steven Barthelmaus, either.

She eased her fingers from his grasp. "Thank you for my daughter and for being here for me."

Speech was becoming increasingly more difficult for Steve as he realized the magnitude of what he'd just shared with Jennifer. They'd witnessed a miracle together and he wasn't ready to let go of the moment. An impatient nod from the medic at the head of the gurney indicated he didn't have much time before Jennifer and the baby would be whisked away from him.

Catching up Jennifer's hand again, he brushed his lips across it before tucking it back to her side. Seeing new life come into the world always moved him, but when that new life was of his own species, the feeling was indescribable.

"Thank *you*, Jennifer. This was an experience I'll never forget," he managed to say through a tight throat as the gurney started to move. "I'll see you soon. I don't think we're done yet, do you?"

Puzzled by his question, Jennifer wasn't sure how to answer. Exhausted physically and emotionally, she merely nodded.

She heard Sue Nelson demanding to see her. The case. It wasn't over. She hadn't gotten even halfway through her questioning of Barthelmaus. That's what he'd been referring to. The hearing would have to be rescheduled, meaning another delay.

What a mess she'd made of things. Her professional side wanted to halt the medics once more so she could talk to Sue. She'd never bailed out of a case, but she was going to have to at least offer to turn this one over to a colleague. She owed her client the opportunity to get her divorce finalized soon.

The warm, tiny body in her arms squirmed slightly and the attorney in Jennifer disappeared. She had her daughter and she was the most important thing in her life. Sue Nelson could wait.

Stephanie. Stephanie Gale Lewis. Julie Ann had been the name she'd picked out, but it just didn't seem right now that the baby was here.

"Stephanie?" Jennifer called softly, brushing her fingertip across the baby's tiny nose. The infant opened one eye, then closed it again with a little sigh of contentment.

Her eyes were blue. She was a Stephanie for sure, Jennifer decided, unable to keep from remembering another pair of soft blue eyes. A lot of babies might be born with blue eyes but she was sure that this baby's would stay that color.

Two

After being run through a gauntlet of doctors and nurses, Jennifer was finally delivered to the peace and serenity of a semiprivate room in the maternity ward. Though physically more exhausted than ever before in her life, she was on such an emotional high that sleep was impossible.

Glancing at the empty bed on the other side of the room, she felt a wave of disappointment. Then she laughed.

She, who'd always guarded her personal life so tenaciously and avoided getting involved in the details of others', wanted to chat away about every intimate detail of her delivery and would be thrilled to hear the same from another new mother. More than anything right then she wanted a good long session of "women talk," that strange thing at which others of her sex seemed so adept and she had always felt so inadequate.

Jennifer laughed again. She'd known her body had gone through a lot of changes in the past several months but she hadn't expected her brain to change every bit as dramatically. The months of her pregnancy hadn't done it, but delivery certainly had.

She eyed the telephone resting on the stand next to her bed. Surely there was someone she could call, someone who'd be willing to listen to her babble about her delivery and the beautiful, little blue-eyed girl she'd brought into the world.

She reached for the phone then brought her hand back. There really wasn't anyone she could call who wouldn't be calling the men in the white coats to come get her immediately after she hung up. She'd done too good a job of holding people at arm's length and making it clear that her business was her own and she didn't appreciate anyone putting their nose into it.

The people at the office, colleagues and staff alike, had tried to get closer to her especially after she'd gotten pregnant, but she'd discouraged any talk about her pregnancy except that she was feeling fine. Of course, to avoid erroneous speculation about the father of her child, everyone at the firm and a handful of her clients did know how Stephanie had been conceived. A few knew the barest of details concerning her reasons for choosing artificial insemination, but she'd avoided any further discussion once the initial explanation had been made.

Feeling an urgent need, and dispelling the last nurse's orders that she call the nursing station for help the first time she used the lavatory, Jennifer eased herself slowly and gingerly off her bed. Her knees nearly buckled beneath her and she grabbed at the bed and waited for the moment to pass. It didn't. She'd never felt so weak in her life.

About to reach for the call button, she almost lost her grip on the bed when a voice sounded from the doorway. "Just what do you think you're doing, young lady?"

A white-jacketed woman wound an arm firmly around Jennifer's waist before she could utter a word in her defense. "You new mamas fall into two categories—the hopelessly helpless or the ridiculously independent," the nurse told her as she eased Jennifer into a nearby arm chair. As soon as she had her settled, she introduced herself as Elizabeth O'Connor, day supervisor of obstetrics.

"Lucky for you I was on my way here to check up on you," Elizabeth said. She wagged a scolding finger at Jennifer, but the twinkle in her blue eyes and the grin on her pixieish face softened the severity of her reprimand. "Now listen here, Ms. Independent, you're going to let us take care of you or I'm going to tie you in that bed."

Unable to help herself, Jennifer giggled. "I'll try to be a good girl." Sheepishly she admitted, "Thanks for the rescue. I overestimated myself."

"Just don't do it again," Elizabeth warned with mock sternness. "I don't like having my patients passing out on the floor. Not good for the hospital's image." She punctuated her sentence with a wink and Jennifer found herself giggling again.

Moments later Jennifer had taken her first "stroll" as Elizabeth called it—the walk to the lavatory and back—and was safely ensconced back in her bed.

"When will they be bringing my baby in?" she asked, crossing her fingers that the answer would be soon.

Elizabeth picked up the chart she'd tossed at the end of the bed when she'd rescued Jennifer. Scanning it quickly, she shook her head. "Probably not for several hours. She's being held in isolation and observation right now."

Panic seized Jennifer with a cold iron-fisted grip. "Isolation and observation? They told me she was okay. Has something developed? What's wrong?"

"Calm down, nothing's wrong," Elizabeth said with a reassuring pat. "This is standard procedure for preemies and especially for ones born outside of the hospital. It's just a precaution."

The nurse read through the chart again to make sure. "According to everything I see here, both you and your baby are doing just about as good as any new mama and baby could be—especially given the circumstances of the birth."

Replacing the chart, the young woman grinned impishly. "Rumor has it you delivered at the courthouse. A judge's chambers no less. Ms. Lewis, how did you manage that?"

The woman's smile and warm nature were infectious and the guards Jennifer usually rallied against strangers took a vacation. Jennifer's newfound feminine need for "women talk" took full control of her consciousness.

Her explanation brought a gale of laughter from the diminutive nurse.

"Well, I'd say a horse doctor's better than a taxi driver. He sounds like quite a guy. What's he look like?"

Memory of Steve Barthelmaus's wondrous eyes, even more wonderful voice and his soothing touch came instantly to Jennifer. A soft sigh escaped involuntarily. Out of the corner of her eye, she saw what looked suspiciously like a knowing grin on her nurse's face. Forcing her voice to sound nonchalant, she shrugged and said, "Actually, he's really not all that outstanding. Pleasant would be a good description."

Elizabeth's grin didn't dim one whit, and Jennifer would have had to have been blind not to guess what the young nurse was thinking and exactly why.

Though it was alleged to be common for pregnant women to fall at least a little bit in love with their obstetricians at the time of delivery, Jennifer was sure she wasn't harboring any such foolish emotion. Steven Barthelmaus was not her obstetrician, and she had definitely not fallen in love, become infatuated, or anything else with the man! So what if he had gorgeous eyes she'd wanted to drown in, hands that had offered both gentleness and security and a voice that had hypnotized her? She hadn't been at all herself this morning. If she saw him again, she doubted he'd have the same effect on her.

"Maybe it's about time I got myself a pet," Elizabeth said when she'd finished marking Jennifer's chart with the latest readings. "Is this pleasant-looking vet single?"

Jennifer frowned, trying to remember everything Sue Nelson had told her about Dr. Steven Barthelmaus. They'd discussed his professional qualifications but nothing about him personally. He could have a wife and six children for all Jennifer knew, but yet something told her there wasn't a brood of little Barthelmauses running around somewhere.

He'd seemed so excited, absolutely ecstatic about Stephanie. Would a man who was a father already be that entranced with somebody else's newborn? She didn't think so. But maybe he was a man who just plain loved babies. Or, maybe in her excitement, she'd imagined the same level of emotion in those around her.

"I don't really know," she answered slowly. Thinking he might have a wife made her feel even more embarrassed over the fantasies she'd built around him during her labor and delivery. Quickly, to overcome her discomfiture, she put her fantasies into proper perspective.

Common sense dictated that just as she'd long ago put away the book of fairy tales that had offered her escape from reality throughout her childhood, she now stored safely away the fantasy that Steve Barthelmaus had been something more than a substitute obstetrician.

"He's probably married," Elizabeth said with exaggerated resignation as she reached for the sphygmomanometer tucked in a wall rack at the head of Jennifer's bed. "Might as well take your blood pressure and see if your little show of independence did any damage."

Wrapping the pressure cuff around Jennifer's arm and pumping up the mercury, she commented, "Guess I won't go out and get a puppy after all. For a minute there, he sounded like somebody I'd really like to get to know. But the good guys aren't usually running around loose and this guy definitely sounds like one of the good guys."

He'd sure acted like one of the good guys, Jennifer thought to herself. Too good to be true.

For a while that day, he'd been everything the Prince Charmings and dashing knights in shining armor were supposed to be—and more. But the living happily ever after ending to this tale did *not* include Steve Barthelmaus whisking her off to his castle. Believing otherwise would only lead to certain disappointment. The real-life ending starred two people, herself and her new daughter, and Jennifer was more than content, for little Stephanie was indeed a dream come true.

Minutes later, after assuring Jennifer that her blood pressure was pretty close to normal and that she ought to try to take a nap, the nurse left her alone. Though taking a good long nap was the sensible thing to do and her body cried out for it, her mind was not yet ready to give up consciousness.

Remembering the look she'd gotten of herself when she'd been in the lavatory, she pulled the hospital table closer, flipped up the built-in vanity and viewed herself again. What hair wasn't standing on end, hung in limp ropes at her shoulders. Any makeup she'd started out the day with had long since disappeared.

She wasn't expecting any visitors and she wasn't particularly vain, but still she didn't want to spend her hospital stay looking like a wild woman. The contents of her purse didn't offer much beyond a comb, a hair clip and a tube of lipstick, but they were a beginning.

Feeling better after she'd tamed her appearance, she eyed with some distaste the drab hospital gown covering her body. The robe Elizabeth had dug out of the closet and draped across the end of her bed was just as institutionally grim. If things had gone as planned, she'd have with her the bag she'd packed only the week before.

She knew she wouldn't be at the hospital long, but still she'd like to have the pretty new robe, slippers and gowns she'd bought just for the occasion along with all her own toiletries. There was also a going home outfit for the baby and a cloudlike blanket to wrap her in. Her own vanity aside, she felt it was imperative to have her overnight bag brought to the hospital. Her baby was not going to leave the hospital in borrowed clothing.

Jennifer reached for the phone again, but without any hesitation this time. There was absolutely no reason to continue being so ridiculously independent as Elizabeth had so aptly called her. As she waited for an answer at her office, she reminded herself that her secretary, Lanine Jones, was a truly sweet young woman. Furthermore she was the mother of two little boys and would certainly understand her request.

Jennifer wasn't disappointed. Before she could ask Lanine to pick up the things at her house, Lanine was volunteering to do just that and anything else Jennifer needed done. What could have been a very short phone call turned out much longer. A host of staff and attorneys present in the office, including the senior partner, wanted in on the chance to extend their congratulations and be assured she and the baby were doing well. Jennifer's newfound need for "women talk" was thoroughly indulged as she supplied the details and vital information about the baby's size and appearance over and over again, as well as confirming the rumor that she'd been delivered by her expert witness, the veterinarian. However, unlike the conversation she'd had with her nurse, she kept any enthusiasm for Steve Barthelmaus safely contained.

For a long time after the phone call, Jennifer lay looking out the window thinking about the conversations she'd just had. It seemed she'd been the talk of the office ever since the call had come in that she was in labor at the courthouse. Yesterday she would have been uncomfortable with that knowledge. Today she felt uncharacteristically relaxed about it, even a little bit warmed by the interest of her associates.

Mr. McMillan, the senior partner, had sounded almost fatherly. He'd always been kind, but maintained a certain distance from the associates and junior partners that made them all, herself included, hold him somewhat in awe. His friendly attitude of today took a little getting used to.

In an attempt to turn her conversation with McMillan toward a professional vein, she'd brought up the Nelson case, intending to offer some suggestions about whom to turn the rest of the case over to. He'd abruptly cut her off with a reminder that she was now on the maternity leave they'd discussed months ago and shouldn't be worrying about anything but herself and her new baby.

"But—" She had started to protest and been cut off.

"Now, now, Jennifer, you're not to worry. You leave that to me," Harold McMillan had told her firmly. "Sue Nelson has already called the office and wants you to know she's willing to wait until you're back before rescheduling the hearing. She assured us her husband was in agreement, but I'm going to give his attorney a call just to make sure. Feel better?"

Jennifer did but only slightly. "It'll be several weeks before I could finish this case up. Will the judge let it drag out that long?"

"Fred Williams and I go back to our law school days. I'm sure he's already categorized this delay under an act of God. We'll get a new date for the hearing." Then he'd chuckled and told her he would have given anything to have seen his old friend dashing around the courthouse trying to find a physician.

He'd finished the conversation saying, "I know how badly you wanted this baby, Jennifer. I speak for everyone here when I tell you we're wishing you every happiness. Take care of yourself and enjoy this special time. In case you didn't notice, you picked a great day to have a baby."

Remembering McMillan's final comments, Jennifer looked at the view out her window with new eyes. It was a perfect day for welcoming a new life. The sky was blue with just a scattering of white puffy clouds. Her room was on one of the towering hospital's middle floors and Jennifer could see the feathery pale green of the treetops, resplendent in their delicate spring beauty. She'd caught a glimpse of a bed of bright tulips and sunny daffodils when she'd been wheeled into the hospital. A light breeze had scattered a cloud of pale pink crabapple petals just as she and Stephanie had been lifted through the ambulance's doors. Fancifully she wondered if the petals had really been fairy dust sprinkled as a blessing on her child.

"Jennifer, your mind has definitely gone wacko," she said aloud as she nestled her head against the pillows. "It's Stephanie's mother who really needs to be put under observation. The woman's slipped off to never-never land."

Never-never land. It had been a very long time since

she'd thought about that magic place depicted in the dog-eared copy of *Peter Pan* that she'd managed to keep with her during her nomadic childhood. Oh how she'd loved reading about Peter, Wendy and all the lost boys when she'd been a child. But it hadn't been to that story's magical place that she'd wanted to transport herself. It had been to the fairy-tale kingdoms of handsome princes and beautiful princesses depicted in a thick book of fairy tales, her other fiercely protected possession. How many nights had she gone to bed, wishing with all her heart that she'd be awakened by the kiss of true love and carried away to a castle on a hill where a big, loving family would embrace her as their own.

"Enough with the fairy tales," she chastised herself as she plumped her pillows and nestled her head against them. "You've done more than enough fantasizing for one day. Steve Barthelmaus is not the handsome prince and you are definitely not sleeping beauty. You're an ordinary mortal woman whose just gone through the most human of all things—giving birth."

She smiled. *She was a mother.* She'd never have a castle on a hill but she did have a family finally. It wasn't a big one, but it would be a loving one and her daughter would always know she'd been wanted and was deeply cherished.

As the afternoon sun slipped lower, Jennifer's body began to relax and her mind gave in to the physical exhaustion of her labors. Gradually she submerged into a restorative sleep where her conscious mind couldn't reject gauzelike dreams and misty fantasy.

She lay on a blanket on the lush grass growing beneath a huge spreading tree covered with pink blossoms. The light breeze was fragrant with the scents of warm earth and spring blossoms. The sun peeked through the blossoms overhead scattering warm patterns on her skin. A bird sang off in the distance.

Beside her was a blond-haired man, murmuring nonsense words to the chubby-legged toddler he held high above his chest. Jennifer rolled to her side and propped her head in her hand, taking in the idyllic scene being played out beside her.

The warmth and joy reflected in the man's blue eyes were matched by the expression and color of the baby's as the tiny little girl babbled in response to the man's softly spoken stream of chatter. Secure and trusting in the big gentle hands that held her aloft, the curly-haired blond baby pumped her little legs and waved her plump arms.

Just as Jennifer joined in with the baby's gurgle of laughing joy, the scene changed. Gone was the blanket beneath the tree, and in its stead was a large room. The furnishings were indistinct save for the brightly decorated fir tree soaring to the high ceiling overhead. Instead of the sun touching her skin, she could feel the warmth from a nearby fireplace.

Song filled the air, but not from a bird. A little girl's voice, a girl of maybe six, reached tentatively for the notes of the simple carol she was attempting to play with fingers not quite long enough or sure enough for the ivory keys stretching out before her. A man's deeper baritone firmly carried the melody, patiently holding one note until the young accompanist found the next. Turning toward the singers, Jennifer saw two blond heads bent toward each other, one with berib-

boned long curls above a lace-trimmed red velvet
dress; the other a darker shade topping a broad set of
tweed-covered shoulders.

Unwinding her ankles, Jennifer started to move to
join them but they faded away, and she knew a moment of terrible anxiety until another scene unfolded.
Laughter, high-pitched squeals and a low rumbling
chuckle filled the air and she relaxed. A pigtailed girl
clutched the handlebars of the shiny new two-wheeler
with determination. Her coltish legs were just long
enough for her sneaker-clad feet to reach the pedals.

Jennifer sensed a touch of fear in the girl's voice as
the bicycle began to move on the pavement. Fear
grabbed at her, too, but only until she caught the
sound of the reassuring words uttered by the man
running alongside the novice biker.

"Easy, easy, girl," he said, one hand firmly on a
handlebar, the other at the back of the seat. "You're
doing fine. I'm right here. Trust me. I never break
promises."

Jennifer tried to get closer to the pair but they
seemed to move farther and farther away. "Come
back," she pleaded, trying to hold on to the hazy images evaporating in the distance.

Other sounds were intruding into the world where
she'd gone for too short a time, and she struggled
against them until she sensed a presence hovering near
her. Reluctantly she opened her eyes.

Once her vision cleared of the foggy dregs left by
sleep, Jennifer scanned her room quickly for the presence she'd sensed. She saw the blond-haired man she'd
seen in her dream moving toward her hospital room
door and she smiled. Feeling as if she were still hang-

ing on to a thread of her dream, she said, "Steve...you *are* here."

"Sorry, I woke you," he said. And with those few syllables Jennifer felt again the comforting security his voice had offered her hours before. He walked slowly back toward her bed, and the happiness she'd felt at first seeing him heightened. Unable to resist, she smiled.

She started to lift her arms toward him, wanting more than anything to be held against his broad chest, feel his strong arms wrapped protectively around her. Shaking her head slightly, she dropped her hands back to the sheets. This was the man who'd been in her dream, but she wasn't sleeping now and had to face the real world.

Steve Barthelmaus had come through for her when she'd desperately needed help. She didn't need his help anymore, and she wasn't being ridiculously independent in assuming that attitude. She was merely being realistic.

"It was nice of you to come." She fumbled with the controls on her bed, keeping her face averted as she wrestled with her reactions to this man as well.

Steve felt as if she'd just slapped him in the face. He and this woman had shared one of life's most miraculous moments and she greeted him with a casual *It was nice of you to come.* That was the understatement of the year!

Nothing could have kept him away. It wasn't every day he helped bring a member of his own species into the world. He wanted to sing, dance, hand out cigars and candy.

Hell, he wanted to pound his chest and bellow the news of little Stephanie's birth for the whole world to hear. Then, having opened the safety valve of that pressure cooker of emotions, he wanted to go reverently to this beautiful woman, hold her and be held by her as together they reveled in the joy of this special day. That's what a man ought to do at a time like this ... if that man were the baby's father.

You're not that man, Barthelmaus. If he'd felt slapped in the face with Jennifer's casual greeting, he felt axed by the truth he'd just remembered.

He was nothing more in this play than a substitute obstetrician, the understudy for what was really a very minor role, and therefore he didn't warrant a love scene of any kind with the heroine. That scene had obviously already been played long before Steve Barthelmaus had come onstage. Though the man who'd co-starred had absented himself before the finale, there was no guarantee he wouldn't yet make an appearance. There was no guarantee, either, that the heroine might not welcome the man's return.

He'd done a little bit of detective work after Jennifer and the baby had left for the hospital. To the best of anyone's knowledge, Jennifer Lewis was not a widow. He'd sensed when he'd queried Sue Nelson that she knew something about the baby's father even though it was obvious that she shared only a professional relationship with her attorney. Still, the case had been going on for months, starting even before Jennifer's pregnancy. It would seem only natural that the pregnancy would be mentioned and that Sue might know something. Her reluctance to give him any details had fortified his theory that the man had just plain walked out on Jennifer.

Holding in check a potpourri of emotions—anger, disappointment, but still a good measure of elation left over from the big happening of the day—Steve waited until Jennifer finished adjusting her bed. Once she was completely sitting up, he asked, "How are you feeling? You and Stephanie okay?"

His use of the baby's name knocked a small crack in the defensive wall Jennifer had thrown up around her feelings. This was, after all, the man she had named her baby after. Flashes of the scenes in her dream went quickly through her mind, and she felt again the warmth and joy in each interlude. Just as quickly she dismissed them to the make-believe world where they belonged.

"We've both been pronounced in perfect health, or at least I have." She couldn't keep the touch of anxiety out of her voice when she added, "Though the pediatrician says the baby is checking out fine so far, he's reserving final judgment for a few more hours. She's over five pounds, but they're still—"

Jennifer's voice broke slightly but she quickly pulled herself together and explained that the baby was being held in isolation for observation.

Steve experienced a moment of cold fear in reaction to this information before a wave of protective rage came over him. He wanted to dash down to the nursery and make sure there were at least four staff members posted around Stephanie's bassinet continuously. Nothing was going to happen to his baby!

No, not *his* baby—Jennifer and that deserter's baby, he quickly corrected. Damn that man! Why wasn't he here?

"Standard procedure for preemies," Steve said smoothly, hoping to ease some of Jennifer's anxiety. *Sure, Barthelmaus. As if you know what standard procedure is for premature human infants.* He would have laughed at his own presumption if he hadn't feared adding to Jennifer's worries.

"Nothing to fret about," he said. "That little girl had one healthy set of lungs when she was born, remember?" He punctuated his words with a chuckle as he remembered Stephanie's angry wailing right after she'd come into the world. He hoped Jennifer remembered, too.

"She was making a lot of noise wasn't she?" Jennifer laughed slightly and Steve felt better. At least he'd eased Jennifer's concerns.

"You're sure you're all right?" he asked again, needing the assurance that he hadn't bungled anything during those frantic moments in the judge's chambers. "I'm no obstetrician, and the judge's chambers wasn't the most ideal place for a woman to give birth."

"I'm fine, really," Jennifer replied, wishing he weren't so terribly concerned about her physical condition. She didn't need his reminder that he wasn't her obstetrician. Now that the emergency that had prompted his substitution was long passed, she was feeling more and more embarrassed in his presence—and not just from the memory of the role she'd cast him in in her fantasies and dreams. During those hectic minutes before the baby had arrived, circumstances hadn't allowed for any modesty or even dignity, and she hadn't really given either a thought.

Now she did.

Remembering all too vividly how intimately Steve Barthelmaus knew her body, how totally out of control she'd been both mentally and physically, and acutely aware of her current near-naked state in a thin open-backed hospital gown, Jennifer sought to create some distance between them. Shrouding herself in her best courtroom persona, she thanked him again for all he'd done for her.

"And thank you again for coming," she added and presented her hand for a very businesslike handshake. "I don't want to keep you. I imagine your family is wondering where you are."

Three

———

Steve stared at Jennifer's extended hand for several seconds. Though it represented contact, the gesture coupled with her words were a dismissal. And not just a simple dismissal at that. Unless his instincts were really off, she was telling him to get out and stay out.

A temper, usually buried so deep it never surfaced, flared within him.

If that's what the lady wanted, that's what the lady was going to get. He knew he wasn't God's gift to the female population, but he knew there were plenty of women who were more than happy in his company. He didn't need to force himself upon a woman.

"I don't have a family waiting for me at home, but I should be getting home anyway," he said offhandedly. Reaching for her hand, he fully expected to do nothing more than clasp it firmly, then let it go. But the moment her small soft palm fit within his much larger one, he remembered how she'd clung to him through her labor. He supposed she might have done that to anyone who'd been there at the time, but his ego wanted to believe there had been some element of discrimination in the way she'd entrusted herself to him.

His temper crawled back into hibernation. Instead of letting go of her hand, he tucked it gently between both of his. He felt a sense of satisfaction and something else that he couldn't label when Jennifer didn't try to pull her hand away.

Years of experience with the nonverbal communication his patients gave him prompted him to revise his interpretation of what this woman's words and tone had really meant. People were, after all, animals. A higher form than he dealt with in his profession, certainly, but they were still animals. And one thing he had learned was that an animal's nonverbal communication was generally more honest than the words humans used.

He'd tapped into instinct or developed a knack over the years for reading all the nonverbal signs animals used to express their feelings. Actions, body language and eyes gave keys to what an animal was feeling. Maybe it was wishful thinking on his part, but something about the way she'd let her hand relax in his told him she wasn't really as anxious to get rid of him as her words might have indicated.

"It's been quite a day, hasn't it, Jennifer?" he said, willing her to look at him. Ignoring her obvious dismissal of him, he launched into a totally desultory nearly one-sided discussion, covering the weather, local news of the day, anything he could think of to stall for time.

Chalking up her reaction to Steve's divulgence that he had no family waiting for him as another example of the insanity brought on by overactive hormones, Jennifer dismissed her feeling of relief and tried again to keep her feelings toward this man in perspective. However the touch of his strong hands and the gentle sound of his voice were having the same effects on her now as they'd had back at the courthouse.

Worse, those features of his she'd tried to deem merely pleasant were putting Robert Redford in the shade. It was the eyes. If only she could avoid looking at them, but the darn things were like magnets pulling her attention no matter how hard she tried to direct her gaze elsewhere. While his eyes were gentle and honest, at the same time they made her feel transparent, as if he could read her every thought.

After watching a parade of emotions march briskly across Jennifer's face, Steve saw again the same look of vulnerability in her eyes he'd seen back at the courthouse. He'd decided right then and there that the comparison he'd made back at the courthouse between her and his cat, Hugger, had been correct.

That haughty little feline had thrown up every show of independence and dignity possible to convince him she didn't need him once he'd gotten her on the road to good health. His every instinct told him that Jennifer was doing the same thing. What's more, he suspected she was just as in need of some sort of help as the cat he'd adopted eight years ago.

Vulnerability wasn't all he saw in the darkly fringed gray eyes looking up at him. He saw a wariness there, too. That was a look he'd seen hundreds of times before. Not in a woman, perhaps, but he'd seen the look in many a skittish animal when he'd first approached.

When you can, let an animal approach you first. No quick moves to scare them off. You have to try to earn their trust first.

He'd heard that advice from his father when he was a small boy on the farm and again years later from his instructors in veterinary school. It was good advice for dealing with animals, even pretty female *homo sapiens* who for some reason didn't trust people very easily. Having never given up on an animal, he was determined to win this woman's trust. Not knowing any other tack to take and encouraged that she hadn't yet pulled away, he continued to hold her hand, stroking it gently and casually as he kept their conversation going.

"Will you have someone to stay with you when you and the baby go home?" he asked, finally having exhausted every other possible topic.

"No, I live alone," Jennifer supplied, then winced slightly when Steve's grip on her hand tightened dramatically.

"You can't go home to no one!" Again Steve forgot all about calm being an important prerequisite to gaining a creature's trust. Imagining Jennifer and her baby going from the security and care of a modern hospital to a totally empty house was totally repugnant.

Keeping her voice firm and steady Jennifer responded, "I can and I will." Internally she was anything but steady in response to Steve's abrupt change in tone and mood. She tried to remove her hand from Steve's grasp. Her efforts proved fruitless for he had a grip on her that rivaled that of a bear trap.

"But you can't," he blurted, totally beyond his ken to imagine a woman being all alone at a time like this, and he told Jennifer so and more.

His sisters, though not Amazons were hale and hearty women. Some people might even liken them to the legendary pioneer types who allegedly dropped their babies in the fields, then picked up the plow to continue the row. Yet they had been treated as virtual invalids for close to a week after they'd given birth. His mother had made sure her daughters had literally not lifted a finger for days after their birthings.

Looking down at Jennifer, he wouldn't describe her as hale and hearty under any circumstances. She looked so fragile and small.

Despite long limbs, she wasn't very tall. His guess was she was less than average height. Sixty-three inches, tops, he figured. Not much weight on her and she was small-boned. Remembering how easily he'd lifted her into his arms and carried her into the judge's chambers, he estimated her normal weigh* was probably not much over a hundred pounds.

If the care given his sisters had been at all necessary, it was mandatory in Jennifer's case and then some. Outrage at the unknown man who'd deserted this woman raised its hoary head within Steve's breast. That bastard had left her alone when she didn't have any family close by. A score of names far worse than bastard came to Steve's mind to describe Jennifer's deserter.

"You just had a baby. You need care. The baby needs care," he babbled, giving vent to his frustration with what he saw as clearly unconscionable circumstances. So the father of her child had skipped and she was without family. That still didn't mean she had to be alone when she and the baby left the hospital. There were people who could be hired to stay with new mothers.

Steve knew just the one. His housekeeper, Marian Jenkins. The woman worked only two days a week for him—when she wasn't caring for one of her many relatives in the county who'd just had a baby or someone, like Jennifer, who had no one. Calming somewhat, he suggested, "I can arrange for someone to come stay with you." The disdainful look he received in response broke the tenuous thread of his last show of calm. "You can't be by yourself!"

"Of course I can," Jennifer snarled back, matching him in volume. Yanking her hand from his grasp, her chin set stubbornly, she dared him to try to touch her again. Her eyes flashed fire, but her next statements were delivered icily. "I am perfectly capable of taking care of my baby. Besides, Dr. Barthelmaus, we're not your responsibility."

The people who knew Steve Barthelmaus as a man of infinite patience and calm wouldn't have recognized the man glaring down at Jennifer. "Look, Ms. Lewis," he began, furious with both her statement and sudden formality. "I helped bring that little baby into the world and you even named her after me. Those two details give me some rights about her welfare and I'm exercising those rights right now. You absolutely cannot be on your own with a newborn baby."

Jennifer sent Steve a look that should have burned him to a crisp. "Look here, you self-righteous busybody, I can take care of myself and my baby. I'm not a child and I'm not helpless and you're not the child welfare department," she stated through clenched teeth.

Steve started to open his mouth in an attempt to defend himself against her accusation, but Jennifer was far from finished. "Neither you nor anybody else has the right to tell me what's best for me or my baby. Not anymore and never again. I'll not be uprooted from my home or my things and neither will my baby."

Feeling the sting of tears at the corners of her eyes, Jennifer made an angry swipe at them. The show of weakness intensified her anger. She knotted her hands into fists to keep them from shaking.

"I have a very nice home to take my baby home to, and I am very capable of providing her with everything she needs and more," she said angrily, trying for a firm tone, but her voice broke slightly on the final words. "I don't drink. I don't do drugs. I have a profession that I'm damned good at so I make a good living. I am a responsible person and nobody—got that—nobody will ever need to step in and take over my baby's care!"

Completely flummoxed by her tirade, Steve saw the tears she couldn't check streaming down her cheeks. He deserved a swift kick in the pants. The last thing he'd wanted to do was upset Jennifer, and he'd just done about as thorough a job as was possible. "Jennifer. I—"

"Just go," she said softly. Emotionally drained, she wearily leaned against the pillows. Turning her back to Steve, she stared out the window while she waited for sounds of his leaving.

Taking a few steps away from her bed, he paused and ran a shaking hand through his hair. He couldn't leave her, not like this.

Panicking and totally blowing his cool had been stupid. She had every right to put him in his place.

That her reactions bordered on hysteria was obvious, but that didn't mean her statements were meaningless. His mind searched for possible reasons that could have prompted some of her statements but turned up nothing that made any sense.

For whatever reason he'd hit a sensitive nerve, but now wasn't the time to press for an explanation. Now was a time for apologies and whatever else he could think of to improve her state of mind.

New mothers, no matter what the species, shouldn't be put through the kind of emotional wringer he'd just unwittingly dragged Jennifer through. All the names he'd thought appropriate for Stephanie's sire were just as applicable to the baby's deliverer.

"I'm sorry," he said quietly. Jennifer didn't move, but then he hadn't really expected two simple little words to do the job. "I was way out of line. I don't know what came over me."

Still no reaction that he could detect from Jennifer.

He struggled against walking around to the other side of her bed so he could see her face. He wanted desperately to read her expression, her eyes, get some clue of her reaction to his apology.

Keeping up a steady stream of talk in what he hoped was the gentlest tone his voice was capable of, he plowed on. "You have every right to call me a busybody. I deserve a lot stronger label than that. I don't know what came over me. Saying I'm sorry seems terribly inadequate, but those are the only words I can offer. I'm sorry, Jennifer."

With each sentence Steve uttered, Jennifer felt the wall she'd thrown up around herself begin to weaken.

Just his tone of voice, that soft but melodious sound that had soothed her from the very first moment she'd heard it, was enough to defuse her temper. He also sounded so genuinely abject.

The combination was irresistible. After mopping her cheeks with the edge of the sheet, she rolled to her back and turned her face toward him. She opened her mouth to say something forgiving, but Steve stopped her.

"Please." Her tear-drenched eyes were so large and so wounded looking, Steve felt as if he'd been stabbed. "I need to say more."

Once again he ran a hand through his hair before shoving his hands into his pockets. "I realize my helping deliver your baby doesn't really give me any rights. All I can say is that it was a helluva experience for me and one I'm sure I'll never have again. Maybe real obstetricians get used to it and are able to separate themselves, but I'm not an obstetrician and it would be mighty hard for me to just walk away from either you or the baby. I really didn't mean to imply that you're incapable of taking care of your own baby. I'm just used to the way it's always been for my sisters when they had their babies and assumed that was the way of things."

He described the way his mother had moved in with his sisters at each of their birthings, hoping Jennifer would understand what had gone through his mind.

Seeing the shadow of an understanding smile, Steve decided to give details of the hours he'd spent pacing the floor with his two brothers-in-law.

"Unlike the men in the family, Mom was always as steady as a rock," he declared. "She always brought her knitting bag to the hospital and calmly sat knitting away with a serene little smile on her face while the rest of us wore down the carpeting. The bigger whatever she was knitting got, the fuller the ashtray got in the waiting room—and none of us normally smoke.''

''Sounds like the men in your family ought to take up knitting,'' Jennifer teased, her mouth turning up at the corners. She'd even laughed a few times, though mirth hadn't yet reached her eyes. If anything, the two big charcoal orbs looked even more wounded than when he'd begun. He'd touched sensitive nerves earlier and he sensed he was still doing it.

In a last-ditch effort to soothe her, Steve stretched his hands, palms up, toward her. Deliberately making them shake slightly, he asked, ''If you think these big things look clumsy, you ought to see Rog and Rick's. None of us would manage even a respectable pile of knots.''

Jennifer looked at the broad palms held out before her and thought she'd never seen more capable hands in her life. Compared to her own, they were big. Calluses on his palms evidenced that they were no strangers to physical work. Big and clumsy? They were big hands but she knew first-hand that they were anything but clumsy.

Though she wanted to discourage any further contact with this man, especially any physical contact, she felt compelled to place her hands atop his. There was so much she could say about the strong palms beneath hers—that his hands could do anything, that they were gentle, skilled, had been a godsend for her that day—but she feared putting voice to those thoughts. In the end, she merely said very quietly, ''Yours are good hands, Steven Barthelmaus.''

"Thank you, Jennifer."

He lifted her hands and brushed his lips across her knuckles. Jennifer felt the feather-light touch all the way up her arm, but couldn't find the will to pull away. For a long moment he held her gaze captive with his own and Jennifer found herself holding her breath. Was it her imagination or was his head moving closer? Her lips began to tingle with excited anticipation while her stomach performed a quick somersault.

But then he straightened, winked and grinned so mischievously, the mood was broken. Jennifer let her pent up breath out as inconspiciously as she could, unsure whether she was feeling relief or disappointment.

"Since you're in a forgiving mood, might now be a good time to ask a favor?"

She eyed him uneasily. "Depends on the favor..." she began. "You're not going to demand rights about *my* baby again, are you?"

Steve didn't miss her emphasis on the possessive and knew he'd better step carefully and slowly. "Will you let me be your friend?"

Jennifer was hard put to keep from letting her mouth drop open. As it was she could feel her eyes widening until they were as big as proverbial saucers. Not really knowing what to say, she heard a voice a lot like her own stammer, "Eh...ah...I think that would be nice."

"Thank you. I think I'll be going for sure now. Will you still be here tomorrow?" he asked as he moved toward the door.

"Probably. No one's given me an exact date for my discharge," she replied, wondering where his question was leading. That his latest query wasn't said just in passing she was sure. There was a look in his eyes that made her nervous.

"That's good. Make them let you stay a few days, if you can. You could use the rest before you get home."

Jennifer smiled warily and thanked him for the concern. "Goodbye," she said as he moved another step closer to the door. He started through it and Jennifer let out the breath she hadn't realized she'd been holding. Just as quickly she caught it again when Steve turned and took a step back into the room.

"Ah...Jennifer...there's one more thing. When you're discharged, would you let me drive you and Stephanie home?"

She'd been shocked by his first request, but it didn't compare to this one. Involuntarily her head began to move from side to side to express her negative reaction. "That's really too much for you to do for me. I...I can have someone from my office come for us...or call a cab...or—"

"A cab...?" Steve's features reflected the same incredulity he'd felt when Jennifer had announced she was going home to an empty house. "You'll do—" Checking himself before he delivered another ultimatum he'd bet his new X-ray machine would cause Jennifer to erupt like a volcano, he forced himself to be calm. "It's not too much for a friend, Jennifer. That's what they're for."

"But I could never repay—"

"Friends don't worry about returning favors. The opportunity just happens. Sometimes big things. Sometimes small." He grinned at her again. "Maybe someday I'll get stepped on by one of my weightier patients and end up with a smashed foot."

Gambling on the soft heart he believed she had, he expanded on the image. "There I'd be with a big heavy plaster shoe, nobody to turn to and stumbling around outside the hospital trying to flag down a taxi with one of my crutches. Alone, in a lot of pain probably, completely helpless...unless my friend came to my rescue." For good measure, he threw in, "You agreed to let me be your friend and I interpreted that to mean you'd be mine, too. Was I wrong?"

Jennifer wasn't sure whether she should laugh, applaud, or throw a pillow at him. And here she'd thought Steven Barthelmaus had the most honest and trustworthy eyes and face she'd ever seen. Ha! The man had the instincts of an old-time snake oil salesman.

Though she felt like the victim of a flim-flam man, she nevertheless shook her head and bought what he was selling. "Okay, okay, I'll be your friend... probably the only one you have," she grumbled sarcastically. "You're such a lousy actor and so pushy, that big family you have has no doubt disowned you and nobody else can stand you."

"Pushy? *Moi?*"

Folding her arms over her chest, she conjured up what she hoped was a stern glare. "Yes, pushy. And most definitely you."

Looking far from contrite, Steve ventured, "See what a good friend you are? You're willing to point out my faults."

At that Jennifer did grab for her pillow and threatened to pitch it his way. "Get out of here, *friend!*"

The mischievous grin was back. "I'll see you soon, my friend," he said and went out the door.

"Not too soon, I hope," Jennifer growled.

* * *

Steve grinned as he looked through the nursery window. Raising his hands, he wiggled his fingers.

The baby being held in a nurse's arms arched one almost invisible eyebrow at him, then yawned, closed her eyes and went back to sleep.

Apparently seeing the look of disappointment on Steve's face, the nurse smiled knowingly as she lay the baby in the bassinet. Then she rearranged the bassinets in the first row before the viewing window so there was room for one more. Rolling the Lewis baby into the space, the nurse looked up at Steve and nodded her acceptance of his mouthed words of thanks.

"Good-looking baby," a male voice sounded beside Steve.

"She's absolutely beautiful," Steve murmured, not taking his eyes from the tiny bundle sleeping a few feet away.

"Mine's the one second to her left. Got a girl this time. The wife's sure happy about it. Third time's a charm, I guess. We already have two little boys."

"That's nice." Steve tilted his head slightly so he could see Stephanie's face a bit more clearly. Unable to help himself, he tapped a finger lightly on the glass, hoping she'd open at least one little eye and look at him, but the baby went on sleeping totally oblivious to the attention she was receiving.

"This your first?"

Almost completely distracted by a small movement of Stephanie's tiny hand, Steve nodded.

"Enjoy. The first is always special plus I've heard little girls really steal their daddy's heart. I guess we're both in for it from these little beauties, pal." The man clasped Steve on the shoulder and moved a few paces away where he, too, began tapping on the glass and grinning at a baby wrapped snuggly in a pink blanket.

Coming to his senses as he listened to the other man babbling total nonsense, Steve realized he'd just claimed Stephanie as his own. He opened his mouth to correct the mistake then decided against it.

All he'd agreed to was that Stephanie was his first. It was a truth, though not the one the man supposed. She was the first baby human he'd ever delivered and he didn't need to be told she was special. As for little girls stealing their daddy's heart, he'd go along with that, too, even if he wasn't this little girl's daddy.

What role he played in Stephanie's life, only the future would reveal. All he knew for sure was that there would be one, for no matter how hard this baby's mother had tried to kick him out of her and the baby's lives, something told him she really didn't want that.

Shoving his hands into his pockets, he continued to gaze worshipfully at the tiny baby girl whose little bald head barely peeped out of a pink blanket. He'd made some headway with the baby's mother. More than he deserved after he'd made her cry.

God, it had felt good to hear her laugh finally. And, she'd agreed to let him be her friend. It was a start, though he wasn't sure friendship was quite the right word to describe what was going on between them.

He stood for a long time at the viewing window, studying the little life he'd helped into the world and attempting to sort out his thoughts. Finally after another quarter of an hour had gone by, he decided it was time to go home.

He still hadn't come up with any sort of logic to explain why he felt so compelled to establish himself in some sort of role in both the Lewis females' lives, but maybe an explanation wasn't necessary. Not yet, anyway.

What was important was setting into motion the plan that had hatched in his mind just as he had been leaving Jennifer's room. Pushy, she'd called him. Whew! Jennifer was going to come up with a stronger term than that when she was confronted with the *fait accompli*. She might even reach for something more threatening than a pillow.

Wavering, he mulled over his idea again before resolving to go through with it. Dammit! The woman needed some help—and she wasn't a stupid woman. She'd come around to accepting the rightness of what he was going to do for her. It was for the baby's good as well as hers. She'd have to see that.

To be on the safe side, he crossed his fingers as he passed through the hospital doors.

Four

———

Jennifer fingered the ruffled lace that edged the hem of the baby dress she'd just unwrapped. The garment, sized specifically for a preemie, looked as if it had been designed for a doll, rather than a real baby. A tiny matching ruffled bonnet nestled in the tissue paper beneath. Turning to her secretary, she blinked away the tears and smiled. "This is the cutest little thing I've ever seen. Thank you."

"You're more than welcome. I had such fun buying that little dress. With only boys of my own, I love an excuse to buy something pink and frilly," Lanine admitted with an easy smile.

"But you've already done so much for me, I didn't expect you to get the baby something, too," Jennifer demurred, feeling overwhelmed. She'd been haunting the baby departments of all the major stores for months and she could guess at the cost of the ensemble her secretary had just given her. Knowing full well what the woman's salary was, she knew the gift had made a dent in her last paycheck. Lanine and her husband had two growing little boys to support plus the recent purchase of a house that stretched their finances to the limit.

Lanine shrugged. "Picking up your suitcase yesterday and bringing it back to you wasn't all that much."

"Well it was to me," Jennifer said, knowing no one could know how important it had been to her to have her own things to put on. Having spent a childhood in hand-me-downs, her college years wearing used and bargain basement specials, she'd vowed her wardrobe would be totally revamped as soon as she'd pulled her first paycheck as an attorney. Little by little, she'd built a collection of coordinated clothing of the highest quality she could afford, including matching shoes and accessories.

Hence, underneath her eyelet-trimmed peach robe was a matching gown. Peach leather mules were on her feet. Not stopping there, after showering she'd used a liberal amount of an expensive but lightly scented body splash and topped off her toilette by winding a peach ribbon through the braid in her freshly washed hair. She felt like a new woman . . . or rather more like the woman she'd become since she'd taken a position at McMillan, Courtney and Wells.

"I'd still be wearing paper scuffs and hospital drab if it weren't for you."

Lanine laughed lightly. "If I may say so, Ms. Lewis, peach does much more for you than that worn out gown you had on yesterday."

''I agree'' sounded a male voice from the doorway. ''You look wonderful, Jennifer, but then I thought so last evening, too.''

Jennifer felt the heat of a blush rise to her cheeks as Steve Barthelmaus sauntered into the room, looking even more handsome than he had the evening before. She could feel her pulse quicken and she didn't like the reaction at all. The man was just a friend, she screamed inwardly, knowing that she was responding to Steve Barthelmaus in ways that went far beyond friendship.

Worse than her hormones' rampaging response was the speculative look on Lanine's face as she looked from Jennifer to Steve. Damn the man! Why did he have to keep showing up here at the hospital?

Unable to avoid it, Jennifer stumbled through the introductions, wishing all the while that Steve hadn't chosen this particular moment to make an appearance. ''Ah... Lanine, this is Dr. Barthelmaus. Dr. Barthelmaus, my secretary, Lanine Jones,'' she said, crossing her fingers that her very efficient secretary would for once have a lapse in her legendary memory for detail.

''Dr. Barthelmaus, it's a pleasure to meet you,'' Lanine greeted warmly. Jennifer knew by the smile on the woman's face and the tone of her voice that her prayer that Lanine wouldn't recognize the man's identity hadn't been fulfilled. Why had she bothered to expect otherwise? No prayer of hers—except for the baby—had ever been answered. She'd given up on them along with fairy tales a long time ago.

''There aren't many white knights roaming around these days. It's a real thrill to finally meet one,''

Lanine announced. "You've become quite a hero at McMillan, Courtney and Wells."

"Well, I'm hardly a hero," Steve responded and Jennifer was gratified to see a tinge of color rise from the man's neck. "Anybody would have done the same thing, given the circumstances."

"Don't be so modest," Lanine chastised. "The way you scooped Ms. Lewis up and carried her out of that courtroom was definitely hero behavior. The way I heard it, everybody else was just standing around gaping, pretty much like a roomful of Prissys from *Gone With the Wind,* claiming they knew nothin' about birthin' babies."

How Lanine knew every detail about what had happened in the courtroom, Jennifer could only speculate. Sue Nelson, her client? Gale Griffith, the judge's secretary? Either could have relayed the information, Jennifer supposed.

The more Lanine went on heaping praise and virtually pinning a medal on him, the more Steve squirmed. Though she knew she should say something to divert Lanine's attention, Jennifer decided to give the woman free rein for a while. Lanine was laying it on pretty thick but it served the man right.

White knight, indeed! If he didn't like the label, then he should stop acting like one. So, he'd "rescued" her yesterday. Fine. She'd been grateful and she'd thanked him. Why couldn't he have left well enough alone?

His first visit yesterday could be classified as polite and she had honestly appreciated it, but anything beyond that was ridiculous and totally unnecessary. She'd agreed to friendship, but he was stretching it a bit far. She'd tried to get that very point across. Furthermore, she'd done everything possible to get him to relinquish the "honor" of driving her and the baby home tomorrow. Just thinking about the skillful way the man had maneuvered her into agreeing to his request made her angry.

As if his visits weren't enough, he'd sent flowers this morning. Not just a simple arrangement, either! The little wicker basket of pink sweetheart roses addressed to Stephanie had been acceptable. In fact Jennifer had to admit she'd been delighted with them. However, the long narrow box containing a dozen long-stemmed pink roses had been a different story.

Like any normal woman she appreciated their beauty and delicate scent—the first she'd ever received. She'd felt a moment of glowing warmth that they'd been sent by such a handsome, caring man. But one moment had been all she'd allowed herself. Roses were like dreams, delicate and quick to fade away. They were to be enjoyed for the moment, then best forgotten.

Glancing at the bouquet resting on the windowsill, she hoped she'd be able to forget their extravagant giver. He'd paid dearly for the blossoms, but so had she. She'd had to spend most of this day explaining to every nurse, aide and member of the housekeeping staff who'd walked into her room that the exquisite bouquet was from a friend—just a friend. Her sharp-eyed secretary hadn't missed them, either, though she'd wisely not commented when Jennifer had claimed once again that "just a friend" had sent them.

Some friend he was. His visits and floral tributes had been embarrassing her for over twenty-four hours. If friends returned favors whenever the opportunity arose, she was returning one in kind. Steve Barthelmaus deserved the embarrassing minutes he was enduring right now. If Jennifer could have thought of any way to extend the session she would have.

Hearing Lanine use the word hero once again gave Jennifer an idea of a way to give Steve several more uncomfortable moments and get rid of him as well. She was convinced he'd taken advantage of her weakened condition yesterday when he'd gotten her to agree to friendship. Now that she knew that his idea of friendship was synonymous with smothering, she was prepared to plea bargain her way to a lighter sentence. She'd plead temporary insanity if she had to, for it was as good an excuse as any she could think of to explain why she'd let this man wheedle his way into her life.

"I'm really glad you stopped by, Steve," she said when there was a pause in Lanine's effusion. "Lanine was about to leave and I was really worried about her going to the parking lot all by herself. You never can be too careful these days, especially after dark."

That it was barely dusk, the hospital's parking lot had heavy security and that Lanine had managed safely earlier, Jennifer hoped neither Steve nor Lanine would think of. "Someone as gallant as Steve wouldn't dream of letting you walk back to your car by yourself, would you, Steve?"

"Well...ah...of course not," Steve was forced to agree, not missing the glimmer of steel in Jennifer's big gray eyes. All he had to do was look past her to see that it wasn't very dark yet and there was already a bright glow from the lights of what he knew from firsthand experience was a heavily patrolled parking lot. He'd just been sentenced to another round of fulsome praise and his judge was enjoying her job.

He didn't know why, but he'd always been uncomfortable receiving praise for having done something he considered basic and purely humane. People invariably did it, and some, like Lanine Jones, got so carried away he wanted to crawl into the nearest hole to escape. He was no hero. He was just a man who'd seen something that needed doing and had done it.

Another glance at Jennifer told him there was no escape and she'd throw a cover over any hole he tried for. "Mrs. Jones, I'm at your service. Ready whenever you are."

Praying she could avert any argument Lanine might present, Jennifer cleared her throat to catch the woman's attention. As soon as Lanine turned toward her, she sent the woman the strongest nonverbal woman to woman plea for assistance that she could conjure. There was a momentary look of confusion on the younger woman's face before she smiled slightly, then began gathering her purse and the folder of letters she'd brought for Jennifer's signature.

Jennifer wanted to shout for joy when Lanine said, "Thank you, Dr. Barthelmaus, I'd appreciate the escort. A woman can never be too cautious when she's out by herself, especially after dark." The woman was so astute. Jennifer made a mental note to see what she could do about getting Lanine a raise as soon as possible.

"Is there anything else you need taken care of?" Lanine asked as she started herding Steve toward the door. "What about your car? It's still at the courthouse, isn't it? I can have one of the firm's messengers pick it up and drive it to your house, if you'd like?"

Her car. Jennifer hadn't even thought about it. "Leave it to you, Lanine, to think of it. I don't know what I'd do without you. You never forget anything," she commented as she reached for her purse and fished out her car keys. About to hand the keys over to Lanine, Jennifer remembered a recent office meeting regarding the tasks messengers were asked to perform. "I don't know, Lanine. Picking up my car is going to involve two messengers and it doesn't fall under the category of legal business. Maybe I'd better think of another way to get it."

Lanine shook her head in obvious exasperation. "Ms. Lewis, really. I know how strict you are about following policy, but this is an emergency and rules can be bent. Even old Hard Nose would approve of this," she surprised Jennifer in saying. "By the way, it was Wells, himself, who made sure you were sent those flowers."

She gestured toward the large basket of assorted spring blossoms before whisking the keys from Jennifer's hand. "Pretty, aren't they? We staff members sometimes think the business manager doesn't have a heart, but it would appear he does. Of course, they're weeds compared to these gorgeous roses, Dr. Barthelmaus."

Steve looked at the bouquet of roses, pleased with what he saw. He'd told the florist they were for a new mother and to make sure they were extra special. "Every new mother deserves a dozen roses," he'd said and meant it, though in all honesty he knew that hadn't been the only reason he'd sent them. He'd hoped the flowers would soften this particular new mother's attitude toward him.

Leaning over, Lanine breathed in the delicate fragrance, then smiled. "I couldn't agree with you more. Ready, Doctor?"

After wishing Jennifer well and assuring her that she shouldn't worry about anything regarding the car or work, Lanine started toward the hallway. "Oh, Ms. Lewis, one more thing. Do you have a child carrier for your car? There are some pretty strict laws about child restraints. The hospital won't let you transport the baby home without an approved baby carrier installed properly in the car." She paused, then looked horrified. "Oh my goodness, how are you getting home?"

The very detail Jennifer had hoped to avoid discussing in Steve's presence! Having a secretary who thought of everything was definitely a mixed blessing. "I know all about the child restraint law," she began, hoping to sidestep the issue of how she was getting home. "I purchased a child carrier weeks ago that fits all the specifications required under the law and then some."

"Good, I won't have to borrow one from my sister," Steve interrupted, effectively answering Lanine's question. "You just tell us where it is and Mrs. Jones and I will figure out the details of getting it into your car. If it's okay with you, I'll use your car to pick you and the baby up. That way it'll be all set up for you when you're able to drive again. That sound all right to you?" Steve asked but Jennifer knew the question was purely rhetorical and didn't bother with a response.

"Oh, Dr. Barthelmaus," Lanine gushed. "You really are a dear. Ms. Lewis is lucky to have you for a ... friend."

Lanine's pause wasn't missed by Jennifer. She'd had no idea the woman was such a romantic and suspected she was quite the little matchmaker to boot. Sending her off with Steve Barthelmaus was a really stupid move!

The tall vase containing Steve's roses was conveniently close. For a brief moment, Jennifer gave serious consideration to committing assault and battery with a vase of flowers. Fortunately for the targets, she wasn't sure whom to aim at—Steve for once again rushing in on his white charger, or Lanine for knighting him for the deed.

Though her hand itched to wrap its fingers around the vase, Jennifer forced it to remain in her lap and did the only thing she could do under the circumstances. "It sounds as if you two have everything under control," she said. She couldn't tack a thank you at the end with anything close to sincerity but managed a weak smile.

"If we don't, we'll work it out on the way to the parking lot," Steve announced cheerily as he guided Lanine out of the room. "See you tomorrow, my friend. Don't worry about a thing, you can count on me."

"But can Stephanie count on me?" Jennifer was paraphrasing silently less than twenty-fours hour later.

True to his word, Steve had arrived at the hospital that morning with plenty of time to spare. As promised, her car was ready and waiting at the curb when a nurse wheeled her and the baby out the hospital's doors. As soon as Stephanie had been secured in the baby carrier in the back seat, they'd started off for the drive home. In a matter of just a few more minutes, she would be walking through her own front door carrying the fragile little life entrusted to her care.

She ought to be thrilled.

She was terrified.

Though she'd been poring over baby-care books for months, had gone to classes during her hospital stay that had covered everything from bathing to burping, she suddenly felt as if she knew nothing. She'd handled and cared for Stephanie as much as possible, but all of this had been done within the secure and supervised confines of the hospital. Though she'd never had to call for assistance, she'd had the security of knowing that the experienced hands of a well-trained nurse had been available to her at a moment's notice.

So lost in her fears, she was unaware of anything else, Jennifer jumped when she felt Steve's hand cover hers. "Didn't mean to startle you," he said, patting her clasped hands lightly. "You'll be okay, you know. I think you're going to be the world's best mother."

"How...how did you know?" Jennifer asked, dismayed that he'd been able to read her thoughts so accurately.

Steve smiled in the gentle reassuring way she'd come to expect from him. "If you hold your hands any tighter, you might cut off the circulation. Assuming it's not my driving, I figure the only thing that's scaring you to death is that tiny baby sleeping in the back seat. I know I'd be scared."

Even if he was lying, his confession made her feel better. As usual, the sound of his voice calmed her nerves. "You didn't perjure yourself in court the other day, did you?" she asked, a smile tugging at the corners of her mouth.

"Don't think so," he said absently as he maneuvered one of the last turns before her street. "Why?"

"Just wondering if you're really a psychiatrist just pretending to be a veterinarian."

"Nothing so fancy as a psychiatrist, ma'am," he said with mock humbleness. "Just an old, country horse doctor."

Jennifer laughed, remembering the image she'd had of what an old, country horse doctor might look like. The man behind the wheel of her car was neither old nor very countrified. Every time she saw him, he looked less like what she'd expected than he had before. Though she assumed he had a collection of durable, washable clothing that he donned each day before meeting his patients, she had yet to see any sign of it.

Beginning with the suit he'd worn in court, right on through to the sports jacket, slacks and polo shirt he was wearing today, he continued to dress as if he were more at home in the city than in the country. However, his easy way of smiling, easier pattern of speech and the soft, yet somehow direct way he had of looking straight at her reminded her of none of the city types she came in contact with each day. And then there was his gentle manner, which drew her like a magnet...except for those times he took an about-face and turned into a pushy know-it-all.

Surreptitiously she studied him. Who are you, really, Steven Barthelmaus? she wanted to ask but kept the question to herself. More to the point, why had she let him maneuver himself into her life? She didn't want or need his friendship, and yet she had it.

Taking his eyes briefly away from the street before him, Steve turned toward her with one of his gentle smiles that tended to make her feel as if all was very right in the world. "Feeling better?"

"A little," she said. She *was* feeling better about caring for her baby, but increasingly less so with her reactions to Steve's presence. Try as she might to convince herself she was irritated each time he appeared, she'd actually felt a surge of gladness and relief when he'd shown up this morning at the hospital.

Allowing herself to depend on this man was a mistake. So he felt some weird sort of responsibility toward her baby and herself. That was now. What about tomorrow, next week, next month? Once the emotional high he was experiencing from delivering Stephanie was over, he'd be gone.

"Good," Steve remarked in response to her answer. Reaching across the console separating the bucket seats in the front of the car, Steve gave her hands another light squeeze. "Everything really is going to be okay, you'll see."

Mentally he crossed his fingers that everything would be okay. Of Jennifer's ability to care for the baby, he had no doubts. The way her face lit up every time she talked about the baby, and the way she'd handled her when she'd dressed her to go home would convince anybody that she loved her child. Loving and truly wanting a baby were, to him, the most essential requirements for caring for a child.

He hadn't exactly snooped, but he'd taken a little tour around her house when he and Lanine had fetched the baby carrier. It had been enough to convince him of two things. One, she lived there by herself. And two, she'd really prepared for the baby's arrival.

The house was small but perfectly maintained and up-to-date. It was furnished well, though to someone like him, living in the house that had been home to three generations and still contained a fair portion of the sundry collections of those generations, Jennifer's house seemed Spartan in comparison. No photos, family mementos, or knickknacks cluttered the surface of even one shelf or table top.

There was an almost sterile look about the place, except for the bedroom she'd prepared as a nursery. Not only did it contain all the necessary equipment— crib, dressing table, etc.—but there were homey touches about the appointments that had looked as if they'd been made by loving hands. Since Lanine had revealed that, to her knowledge, Jennifer had no family, he could only surmise that she'd made the curtains, rocker cushion and crib quilt herself.

No, he had no concerns about Jennifer's taking care of the baby, once she was really on her feet. It was the surprise waiting for her that he was concerned about. Her secretary had thought it was a good idea, and Steve could only hope the woman knew her employer better than he did. Somehow, though his every instinct had told him he'd done the right thing, those same instincts were now telling him that Jennifer was going to think just the opposite.

Turning into the driveway in front of her pretty little Cape Cod styled house, Steve brought the car to a stop behind two others already parked there. The truck she supposed was Steve's. The other vehicle, a medium-sized station wagon, she recognized as Lanine's and wasn't really surprised to see it there.

In just two short days, Lanine had gone from an indispensable secretary to an indispensable friend.

Their relationship having undergone such a change, Jennifer realized it was just like Lanine to want to be in on the homecoming.

Whereas, that same short time ago, Jennifer would have resented the intrusion on her privacy, today she welcomed it. She hadn't really wanted to walk into an empty house. Plus, there was Steve Barthelmaus to consider.

She knew better than to expect the man to just drop her and the baby off, then leave. Not the way he'd been hovering over her and the way he'd been so insistent that she needed someone to stay with her. Without Lanine there to run interference, who knew how long the man might think he ought to stay? He'd probably roll out a sleeping bag and stay all night, she answered herself.

Steve was just helping Jennifer out of the car when the front door flew open and Lanine sped across the short walk to the driveway. A camera dangled from a strap around her neck. "Smile, new mother," she ordered. "Got to get this recorded for posterity. Great looking dress, Ms. Lewis."

Unused to flattery, especially from her secretary, Jennifer wasn't quite sure what to say. "Er... ah...thank you." She'd wanted to look special this day, even if the one she most wanted to impress—her baby—wasn't even aware of all the extra pains her mommy had taken to look good. Years from now, thanks to the pictures Lanine was taking, maybe she would and know just how wonderful her mother thought this day was.

Jennifer had bought the periwinkle silk shift with the matching low-heeled shoes expressly for this homecoming, knowing the color was flattering and hoping she'd be able to fit into it after delivery. It was waistless but it had a belt she could wear once she had a real curve again. Still, it was cut much straighter than the voluminous garments she'd been wearing for several months. She'd been delighted that it skimmed easily over her hips when she'd put it on this morning.

Lanine kept up a steady stream of patter while she snapped frame after frame, recording every facet of the baby's transfer from the car to the house. "Doesn't it feel great to wear regular clothes? You're really one of those lucky ones whose figure snaps right back instantly."

Steve was thinking along the same lines as he walked behind Jennifer, carrying her suitcase in one hand and juggling cartons of sample baby paraphernalia provided by the hospital in the other. He'd had a little trouble keeping from gaping this morning when he'd walked into Jennifer's room.

He'd thought from the start that she was a very pretty woman, but this morning he'd amended that assessment to gorgeous. She'd fastened her hair in a chignon at her nape, much the way she'd worn it in the courtroom that first day...was it really only two days ago? But she'd left a few tendrils loose around her face, a face that had been glowing with health and happiness. Her lips had looked so invitingly soft, pink and moist, he'd had trouble keeping from covering them with his own.

Her lips hadn't been the only enticing part of her. Her pregnancy and then the long robe she'd worn at the hospital had hidden a knockout body. If it looked this good just two days after delivery, he could imagine how fantastic it would be in another month.

He'd been having trouble defining his attraction to Jennifer for the past two days, but not what he was feeling today. Lust. Honest, straightforward lust he hadn't felt in years. Lord, he'd like to wrap his arms around her and press her lush curves tightly against him.

As quickly as the thought had formed, he squelched it with a firm reminder that if he ever hoped to have any place in little Stephanie's life, the worst thing he could do right then was put the moves on her mother. He and Jennifer had built a friendship of sorts and he'd had to do some fast talking to get her to agree to even that much.

Beyond his concerns for Jennifer letting him see Stephanie was his concern for Jennifer herself. From the very beginning he'd sensed a vulnerability about her. She'd been hurt, badly. He doubted he'd be wagering on a long shot if he bet everything he owned that the man who'd fathered Stephanie was the reason Jennifer was so wary.

Right now she needed a friend, someone to take care of her, and that caring didn't include sweeping her into his arms and letting her know what a desirable woman she was. Still, his noble intentions were difficult to remember as he watched the gentle sway of Jennifer's hips as he followed her up the short curved sidewalk. Don't even touch her, he warned himself and was thankful for the burdens filling both his hands.

With the baby in her arms, Jennifer stepped inside her own living room. Her home and now Stephanie's, too. She took a slow walk around the cream, coral and jade room, taking in every item as she gazed around her. Everything was there. Nothing had been taken away. It was a fact she never took for granted even if it had been a lot of years now since her world had been continually uprooted and her things snatched away from her.

Everything was exactly as she'd left it Monday morning, except for one detail. Mouth-watering aromas were wafting from the kitchen, and her dining room table was already set for... four?

Unconsciously clutching the baby a little more snugly to her, Jennifer turned slowly toward Lanine and Steve. "Who else is here?"

Jennifer's big gray eyes had taken on the look of a frightened doe, and Steve almost groaned aloud. Before he could form an answer, Lanine took over. "Dr. Steve has the most wonderful surprise for you." Taking the camera from around her neck, she placed it on an end table.

Holding out her arms, Lanine ordered gently, "Here, let me get my hands on this beautiful little princess for a few minutes. You sit down anywhere you think most comfortable and prepare yourself for the most wonderful lunch your tongue has ever had the pleasure to taste."

Not really giving Jennifer much choice, Lanine carefully scooped the baby from her. Turning to Steve, she ordered, "She's your surprise. You do the introductions."

Five

"Jennifer, I'd like you to meet Marian Jenkins, my sometimes housekeeper but always terrific cook," Steve supplied as soon as a rosy-cheeked older woman bustled into the dining room. "It's Marian we have to thank for that wonderful smell filling the air."

Feeling really nervous now that his moment of revelation had arrived, Steve stalled. "Just what have you been cooking up, Marian? Is that your famous Friendship Cake baking?"

"You know good and well it is," Marian answered. "Just yesterday you practically got down on your knees and begged me to bake one. But that's the only one of your favorites I fixed up for today. This lady doesn't need a heavy beef stew after eating all that hospital food. I figured a good fresh fruit salad and a broiled chicken breast would hit the spot a sure sight better. If that isn't good enough to stick to your ribs, then that's just too bad. This luncheon is in the new mother's honor."

After fixing Steve with a stern eye, she turned to Jennifer, her face breaking into a kindly smile. "I sure am glad to meet you, Ms. Lewis. Steven B., here, can't seem to talk about much else these days except you and that beautiful baby."

Smiling broadly when she took a good long look at the baby in Lanine's arms, she announced, "She's a keeper, that's for sure. Just look at those big blue eyes. Prettiest baby Steven B.'s ever delivered." She turned her attention back to Jennifer. "Lunch is ready whenever you say the word."

Having felt a wave of weakness right after she'd turned the baby over to Lanine, Jennifer had sunk into the comfortable softness of one of the overstuffed armchairs that faced her sofa. Thinking the sooner lunch was over, the sooner all these people would leave her in peace, Jennifer mumbled, "I think now would be fine."

She started to rise, intending to take one of the places already set at the table. But her legs still felt like jelly, her hands were shaking, and she could feel the sting of tears behind her eyes.

"Now, now, you just stay put," Marian placed a gentle but staying hand on Jennifer's shoulder. "Steven B., you bring that ottoman over here so's Ms. Lewis can prop her feet up. I imagine she's feeling plumb tuckered with all the excitement of comin' home and all."

Jennifer didn't argue with the older woman's estimation nor did she shrug off the caressing hand that had remained on her shoulder. She hadn't the strength to do any battle. Suddenly everything was so overwhelming. The awesome responsibility of the baby was one thing, and having had to burden others to do things for her quadrupled her feelings of inadequacy.

Furthermore, knowing her home had been entered by near strangers while she'd been gone made her feel that her very privacy had been invaded. Everything was out of her control, the control she'd fought so long and hard to achieve. A side of her wanted to angrily order everyone out, while at the same time she wanted to thank them for their kindness.

Looking first at Mrs. Jenkins, then at Lanine busy cooing to her baby and finally at Steve dutifully following his housekeeper's orders by lifting the heavy ottoman from its customary spot before her fireplace across the room, she burst into tears.

"I...I'm sorry...I don't know...what's come over me," she stuttered through the flood of tears pouring down her cheeks and the sobs tightening her throat. She covered her face with her hands, embarrassed by her emotional display. But the harder she tried to stop, the more freely her tears flowed. "I...never...cry."

"There, there, darlin'." Marian slipped her arm around Jennifer's slender shoulders. Cradling Jennifer against her bosom, she calmly directed Lanine and Steve, "You two run along. I s'pect visitors'll be welcome maybe tomorrow or tomorrow night."

With a knowing nod, Lanine started toward the nursery with the baby. She gave one of Jennifer's knees a pat as she passed by her. "Don't you worry, Ms. Lewis. My husband thought we needed flood insurance every time we brought one of our babies home."

The assurance didn't do a thing toward stemming Jennifer's tears though she was grateful for the sentiments. "Th ... thanks Lanine. I ... I'll ... call ... you ... tomorrow about ... that ... brief ... for the Thompson ... versus ..."

"Don't you dare," Lanine admonished. "You're on maternity leave. You just rest and enjoy this little dolly."

"Steven B., you get on out of here, too," Marian ordered as she caressed Jennifer's back and rocked back and forth.

"But..." he started to argue, then closed his mouth when Marian fixed him with a quelling glare.

"Aren't you always isolatin' the mares after they've foaled? You know better'n any man that new mamas need peace and rest more'n they need anything else."

"But I can help," Steve offered, his frustration obvious in the tight set of his mouth. He was the one who'd made the arrangements for Jennifer and the baby's homecoming and now he was being summarily dismissed.

"Then start by putting that thing down and get on out of here," Marian told him, reminding him he was still holding the heavy ottoman. "And another thing. Don't you be coming around here again until sometime tomorrow evening, and only if you call first and Ms. Lewis says it's okay. You got that, boy?"

"Yes, ma'am," Steve said, though not at all meekly.

Despite her uncontrolled tears, Jennifer felt a chuckle ripple past the lump in her throat. Maybe there was something in Delaware County's water that made people pushy. Marian Jenkins was a take-over type just like Steve, but unlike her reaction to Steve's maneuvering, Jennifer was grateful for Marian's.

Willingly she gave herself over to the older woman, and magically her tears receded as Marian helped her from the chair and started toward her bedroom. "Come on, honey. Let's get you out of this pretty dress and into a nice comfortable nightie. A nice long nap in your own bed's what you need."

Tucked into bed by Marian's gentle hands, lulled easily into sleep by the lullaby the woman crooned to the baby in the next room, Jennifer slept, her mind drifting through a dream she hadn't had in years. In it were memories of the woman who'd been her mother for only six years. She heard the sound of a woman's voice, sometimes talking softly, sometimes singing. Her scent, an elusive fragrance Jennifer couldn't describe when she was conscious, seemed to envelop her. And finally she felt a touch. Light, yet firm, and always conveying warmth, security and most of all love.

Though she'd suffered years of being shuttled from one home to another, been told all too many times she was a burden, for her first few years of life she'd been loved and wanted, just as her little daughter was loved, wanted and cared for.

A sense of cold, loneliness and worry overcame the dream, and Jennifer awoke with a start. Stephanie!

Throwing back the covers, she practically ran toward the bedroom next to her own. Her heart pounding, she pushed the door open and stepped inside. Stephanie was sleeping soundly in her crib.

Gently she picked up her baby, settled her against her shoulder and lowered herself into a wide-armed rocker.

Content to hold her sleeping daughter close, Jennifer mulled over the scene that had transpired earlier in her living room. She smiled when she recalled how Mrs. Jenkins had called Steve "Steven B.," then later "boy." The woman had obviously known Steve for years, probably since he was little. She might be his housekeeper, but she didn't hesitate to put him in his place.

Suddenly Jennifer realized that Steve was the reason Mrs. Jenkins was here. He just couldn't take no for an answer! What a low-down, sneaky, pushy, know-it-all! If she needed any help, she'd get it herself!

Fighting the anger rising within her, Jennifer carefully placed the baby down in her eyelet-draped bassinet. "I'll get him for this," she mumbled under her breath as she detoured into her bedroom and grabbed her robe and slippers before making her way toward the kitchen. "How dare he!"

"Somethin' bothering you, Ms. Lewis?" Marian asked when Jennifer entered the kitchen.

Now that she was facing Marian Jenkins's grandmotherly countenance, some of the anger drained from her. It wasn't this kindly woman's fault Steven B. had completely overstepped the boundaries of friendship, common courtesy and a string of offenses her legal mind was fast compiling. Taking a calming breath, she said, "Well, yes there is. I think there's been some sort of misunderstanding."

Marian nodded as she picked up a tray from the counter. "Well, best get things cleared up before they fester into something major. You feel up to eating at the table, or would you rather be in one of those nice, big chairs you got in your living room?"

"The table would be fine," Jennifer said, though she doubted she'd be able to eat a bite. Gingerly lowering herself onto one of the lightly padded chairs that surrounded her dining room table, she motioned Marian to join her.

"He didn't clear it with you about my staying with you for a few days, did he?" Marian opened bluntly, apparently unruffled by her charge's glower.

"I'm afraid he didn't," Jennifer said tightly.

"Always was a bossy sort," Marian said, pushing a napkin-lined basket closer to Jennifer. "Blueberry muffins." She took a sip of the iced tea she'd served herself. "Yes, Steven B. gets a bit too puffed up with what he thinks is right, but for all his faults he's a caring kind of person. Never could resist any creature he thought was hurting or helpless. Trouble is, he don't always know when to back off."

"That's for sure," Jennifer agreed. The warm-scented muffins were irresistible, and despite thinking she couldn't eat a single bite, she reached for one and started buttering it.

Marian smiled approvingly as first a muffin disappeared and then some of the fresh fruit compote she'd prepared. "Why I remember when he was around seven and he found this little wild rabbit he was sure was an orphan. That little critter could've fended for itself just fine, but nobody could convince Steven B. of that."

Completely distracted by the story of a very young Steve and the wild baby rabbit, Jennifer cut into the chicken on her plate. By the time Marian finished relating how Steve's father had finally convinced the young boy that what the animal needed most was freedom, Jennifer had finished every morsel on her plate. "He means well, but a body might say he's the kind that comes close to killin' with kindness."

"Do any of his patients survive his *loving* care?" Jennifer asked sarcastically as she drained the last of the tall glass of milk Marian had served her.

Marian laughed. "They manage. He did learn a thing or two in veterinary school, and he grew up some. He just has relapses every so often."

Jennifer rolled her eyes. "Humph," she muttered. "I'm not helpless nor am I an invalid. I can take perfectly good care of myself."

"You sure can."

"I can take care of my baby, too."

"I know you can. You want anything else? Some dessert?"

"Not right now, thanks. Maybe later. I really don't need anyone to stay here with me."

"Sure doesn't look like it," Marian agreed, coming around the table. "You've got a nice little house here. Real handy. Everything on one floor so you don't have any stairs to contend with. A new mother shouldn't be going up and down stairs much for the first week or so. And she shouldn't be driving or pushing a heavy vacuum sweeper, neither. Shouldn't lift anything heavier than her baby, really. But I'm not telling you anything you don't already know, right?"

"Right," Jennifer said firmly, though she wasn't being entirely truthful. She didn't recall being warned against vacuuming or driving, but realized the sense behind avoiding the activities for a week or more. She lifted her feet up as Marian scooted the ottoman beneath them, then wondered when she'd decided to move to the living room and just how she'd gotten there.

Marian's features weren't giving anything away but Jennifer knew she'd just been very slickly outwitted.

Whether she'd thought so or not, Marian had apparently decided she'd been sitting on a straight chair long enough.

Jennifer grinned at the older woman. "Pretty smooth, Mrs. Jenkins."

Marian just shrugged. "Can I bring you anything now that you're all settled?"

Jennifer started to turn down the helpful offer, but she was so comfortably ensconced, the thought of moving was totally repugnant. "The newspaper and the TV's remote, please. But, those are the last things you have to get for me, Mrs. Jenkins. You've been very kind, but I really don't need anyone to stay with me."

"I know and I'll be going soon," Marian told her as she placed the requested articles at Jennifer's elbow. "But I'm going to fetch you a tall pitcher of ice water before I go. Hospitals are the driest places. I never can get enough water after I've been in one. How about you?" She started toward the kitchen. "Sure you don't want me to bring you a piece of my Friendship Cake now, so you don't have to move again for a while?"

Jennifer couldn't say no. The woman sounded too hopeful. "That would be nice, thank you."

Stifling a yawn, she settled more comfortably into the chair and opened the newspaper. Scanning the headlines, she discovered not much had really happened since she'd last read or heard the news. Her personal world had changed dramatically, but the world beyond was going along pretty much the same.

Leafing through the paper for something interesting to hold her attention, she snuggled her head against the chair's back. The next thing she knew she was startled by the sound of her baby's cry, coming from the bassinet that had materialized beside her chair.

Coming fully awake, she swung her legs to the floor and stood. "Mrs. Jenkins?" she called as she scooped Stephanie up and started for the nursery.

There was no answer. The woman had evidently left sometime after Jennifer had fallen asleep. Glancing over her shoulder, Jennifer saw a pitcher of water and a plate holding a piece of cake resting on the table beside her chair. She had only a vague memory now of Mrs. Jenkins placing them there and saying something about leaving her number near the telephone in the kitchen. Had she imagined it or had the woman kissed her forehead before she'd left?

"I think she did, Stephanie," Jennifer said as she gently laid the baby on the dressing table. "She must've given you a little ride, too. That was really considerate of her, moving your little bed in next to me, wasn't it?"

Stephanie was more interested in gnawing on her fist between squalls than giving her mother any revelations about how she and her bassinet had gotten to the living room.

Jennifer's hands began to shake as she realized she'd gotten exactly what she wanted—solitude. There was no one in her house except herself and one very tiny two-day-old baby. A two-day-old baby who was very wet, very hungry and was rapidly losing patience with her mother's amateurish attempts to get her dry. Her complaining grew louder and more strident when her mother decided she needed more than a diaper change before her supper. By the time Stephanie was attired in a fresh little gown, Jennifer was fighting back her own tears.

It was only the first of many small cries that occurred through the ensuing hours. By 3:00 a.m. Jennifer was slipping into the last robe she owned that hadn't been thoroughly anointed with baby formula. Stephanie's wardrobe and linens were nearing a dangerously low level as well.

Nearly staggering with exhaustion, Jennifer managed to get a load started in the washer before the baby woke up again. "You're dry and you kept your last meal down, so you can't be hungry," she told her as she picked up the squalling infant. When rocking didn't soothe the child, Jennifer tried walking the floor, humming any tune she could think of.

She walked what seemed like miles, sang or talked until her throat was sore. "You're just having trouble adjusting to new surroundings," she told the baby. "Everything will start feeling all right tomorrow." The words were an assurance to herself, and she tried desperately to believe them.

During her travels around the house, she swung repeatedly past the piece of paper with Marian's telephone number tacked onto the small bulletin board beside the kitchen wall phone. She was tempted to place the call but managed to resist. Calling someone, especially someone she barely knew, in the middle of the night just wasn't something she felt able to do.

"We'll make it, baby. We'll make it," she repeated before lapsing into another of the one-sided conversations she'd been carrying on throughout the long night. "Your mother's a ridiculously independent type and both of us are paying for it. We both wish Mrs. Jenkins was still here. Steven B. was right, but don't you dare ever tell him so."

Six

Juggling two large hampers heavy with foodstuffs, Steve tapped lightly on Jennifer's door and huddled under the small roof over her front step as he waited. Though it was midafternoon the sky was dark and the rain was coming down pretty steadily. There was a slight chill in the air. Over all, it was a gloomy day. Steve struggled to keep the weather from intensifying the dark mood he was in.

Damn the woman! He rapped again and leaned closer to the door, as much to listen for any sign of an answer as to ward off the rain beginning to blow in sheets against the house.

He waited another minute or two, then tapped the doorbell button. He didn't want to make too much noise, in case the baby was sleeping. When there was still no answer, he pressed the button longer and harder. Shifting the hampers' handles into one hand, he turned up the collar of his trench coat. He swore under his breath when his action sent a trickle of water down his neck.

Where the hell was she? Her house wasn't that big! She should have answered by now...unless something was wrong. Images of Jennifer lying unconscious on the floor and the baby so weak she couldn't even cry, painted themselves vividly in Steve's mind. He started alternately pounding on the door with his fist and blasting the doorbell. He almost fell into the house when the door jerked open.

"What are you doing here?"

"Where were you?"

The demands were delivered simultaneously, the tones identical in their anger. The scowls completed the matched set.

Relieved to see Jennifer alive and conscious, Steve was the first to recover. "Can I come in? It's cold and wet out here."

Jennifer's scowl didn't lessen, though she did move aside so Steve could enter. "Keep your voice down," she whispered. "I just got the baby asleep—finally!"

Setting the heavy hampers on the floor, Steve shrugged out of his coat and hung it on the coat tree near the door. He ran his hand over his wet head, dried his palm on his pants, then took a good look at Jennifer. Her eyes were red rimmed and dark shadowed. Her hair was hanging in a tangle down her back. Her skin was pale.

"You look terrible," he growled, though not terrible enough to him that he wasn't having a rough time keeping himself from pulling her into his arms and kissing some color back into her cheeks and mouth. She was wearing a burgundy velour robe today and it was as attractive on her as the peach one she'd worn at the hospital. The garment was utterly shapeless, and yet the fabric draped over her in such a way his hands itched to seek out the curves hidden beneath.

He'd had trouble thinking of anything but the baby and her since the birth. When desire had entered into his feelings for Jennifer, with the precision and sharpness of an expertly wielded scalpel, his turmoil had doubled. Growling at her seemed a justifiable release for his torment.

He'd spent a restless night tossing and turning, cursing himself for so exclusively dividing his time between his practice and helping train the pacer he co-owned with his father, that he'd let his social life slip to nil. It had been a long time since he'd enjoyed an intimate relationship with a woman. That had to be the reason why he was feeling so edgy, and as easily excited as a stallion in the vicinity of a mare in heat. He hadn't thought of himself as a man who needed to have a woman at regular and frequent intervals, and the possibility that it might be so wasn't helping his mood.

"Thanks a lot," Jennifer snapped after she recovered from Steve's negative assessment of her. For a few seconds, she'd actually felt a surge of joy when she'd discovered that it was he pounding her door in. How dare he act so nasty. She didn't need to be reminded that she was a wreck. Dressed more casually than she'd ever seen him, in faded jeans and a loden-green cotton sweater, he was devastating, and she felt angrier still that he looked so good.

Needing to occupy his hands with something other than Jennifer Lewis's lush body, he picked up the hampers and started toward the kitchen. With each step he felt logical reason begin to return. Surly behavior wasn't the way to win any creature over, least of all a woman. Using consistent kindness and gentle ways was the procedure, he soundly reminded himself. And plenty of it.

"Rough night?" he asked, his voice considerably more pleasant now that he was thinking more rationally.

"We survived." Jennifer braced herself for some sort of retaliatory "I told you so," or a lecture on her foolishness for sending Mrs. Jenkins home. When none came, she followed Steve as he strode straight through her house as if he owned the place.

"Just what are you doing?" she demanded angrily, though careful to keep her voice at a low volume. That wasn't so difficult to do as her throat was nearly raw from all the singing and talking she'd done all night and half the day.

"Marian said your cupboards were pretty bare." He started shoveling plastic containers and ceramic casserole dishes into Jennifer's refrigerator. "She was right. There's practically nothing in here except the leftovers from yesterday's lunch."

Lack of sleep didn't help Jennifer control her anger. "You can just put all that stuff right back in the hampers and take them back to wherever they came from."

"Don't be ridiculous. You'd starve and then Marian would have my head. Besides, she's been up since the crack of dawn cooking up a storm."

"I was planning on calling a grocery and having some things delivered."

Sending her a disarming smile that came dangerously close to breaking down her resistance, he announced blithely, "Now there's no need. You're set up for at least two weeks."

"But . . . but I can't accept all this food. I hardly know Mrs. Jenkins. This is too much. Please, take it back."

"Can't do that. The ladies would be insulted," he said absently as he unloaded the contents of the second hamper onto the counter.

"What ladies? You only mentioned Mrs. Jenkins. Who else is in on this?"

"Just Marian and my sisters."

"Your sisters?" Jennifer was dumbfounded. Total strangers were now sending her care packages. "Now who's being ridiculous? I can afford food. I am not a charity case."

"It's not charity. People where I come from always send food when there's a new baby in the house. Economic circumstances are not a factor."

"But I don't come from where you come from," Jennifer argued.

"Makes no difference. Consider yourself an honorary Delaware Countian, if it'll make you feel any better. Marian and my sisters figure it's the least they can do since you won't accept any other kind of help."

There it was, the dig she'd been waiting for. "The baby and I are getting along just fine. We don't need any help," she stated, but her argument sounded false even to her own ears. She'd come very close to calling Marian Jenkins. Another night like the one she'd just spent and she definitely would.

Ignoring the show of independence he was coming to expect from her every time someone tried to make her life a little easier, Steve hitched a hip on the counter. Reaching for one of the containers he'd placed there, he flipped off the top. "Want one?" he asked, holding up a chocolate chip cookie. Jennifer shook her head, so Steve popped most of the confection into his own mouth. "These are from Karen. Her cookies are even better than Mom's."

Watching the cookie disappear, Jennifer changed her mind. "Maybe I will have one."

Having come to grips with his own anger, Steve smiled. "How about a big glass of milk to go with it? Marian made me pick up some on my way over. I got a gallon in case you felt like sharing these."

In spite of herself, Jennifer chuckled. "You didn't by chance put in a special request for those cookies did you?"

Grinning sheepishly, Steve reached for another cookie. "My sisters take pity on their starving little brother from time to time."

Jennifer openly perused Steve's sturdy body. An inch or two under six feet, he wasn't a big man, but he wasn't little, either. There wasn't any flab on his heavily muscled frame that she could detect, but he was far from lean. He was built like a linebacker. "Starving, hah!"

Shaking her head, Jennifer started toward the cupboard where she kept her glasses. Catching her shoulder gently, Steve halted her. "Let me get the glasses. You go sit down somewhere comfortable and prop your feet up."

"It's my house. You're the guest. I'll do it," Jennifer argued, though being waited on again sounded very good to her. She'd had next to no sleep throughout the night and her body felt achy all over. When Steve had arrived, she had just been about to take a couple of analgesics and climb back in bed to rest as long as Stephanie would let her.

Placing his hands on her shoulders, Steve turned her toward him. He nudged her chin up slightly and took a good look at her. "Don't fight me on this, Jennifer. You really do look beat."

"Thanks again, Dr. Barthelmaus. You really know just what to say to make a woman feel good." She knew from his tone and the look of concern on his face that this time his honest assessment was well-meaning. Still, she hadn't tried to keep the sarcasm out of her voice. She was trying too hard to keep from leaning into him.

Standing almost toe to toe, she realized it would take only a small shift in position to let her body rest against his and maybe feel his arms wind around her. He looked so strong, so dependable, and his big warm hands felt so good as they gently massaged the tightness across her shoulders.

"I'm sorry for being such a bear earlier. I panicked when you didn't answer right away. Baby keep you up all night?" he asked, wanting to hold her and give her some of the nurturing she'd obviously given throughout the previous night and most of the day. Instead he kept his hands at her shoulders, running his fingers and palms over the tightness there, careful to keep his touch light so as not to bruise her.

"This feel better?" he asked, wanting to do much more than just massage her shoulders to comfort her. She looked like a woman who desperately needed some cuddling and he was just as desperate to be the man doing the cuddling.

"Hmm…" Her eyes closed, Jennifer gave in to the magic of his touch.

Encouraged, Steve nudged her a little bit closer. Careful not to spook her he strayed a little bit farther down her back and arms with each sweep of his hands until he'd effectively folded her into a light embrace. His intent was to soothe. Jennifer's low murmur of pleasure indicated he was successful. However his own body was becoming more and more tense as his hands familiarized themselves with the texture and contours beneath his palms.

He tried to divert his mind to something other than Jennifer's soft warm body separated by only an inch or so from his. Standing this close to her, he was struck again by how small she really was. The top of her head came up to only his chin. Breathing deeply, he savored the scent of the fragrance she favored. Expensive but light. Whatever it was it was so alluring it had been haunting him since the moment he'd scooped her up in the courtroom. She was everything feminine beckoning, unwittingly and innocently, to all that was masculine in him.

Ease *her* tensions man, not your own, he warned himself. "I don't know about you, but I'm ready for something a lot heartier than cookies and milk. It's been a long day."

"Your patients give you a rough time today?" Jennifer asked as she brought her hands up to rest against Steve's chest. Her head followed. What could it hurt, she asked herself, to give in to the luxury of being held just this once?

Steve had asked to be her friend, and by his definition friends did things for each other in times of need. His holding her and rubbing the aches out of her shoulders were nothing more than other examples of friendly deeds . . . weren't they? If her body was sending her signals that weren't remotely akin to a reaction to a friend's presence, it was just another example of her out-of-kilter hormones acting up again.

"I had to spend most of the morning in surgery patching up a cat hit by a car," he said, surprised that speech was at all possible. "That put me behind, and just as I was almost caught up, I got called out of the office to stitch up a bull who'd tangled with some barbed wire. He wasn't very happy about having his business parts messed with."

"Business parts?" Jennifer lifted her head slightly.

"He's a prize stud bull. What do you suppose his business parts are?"

Jennifer's eyes widened with understanding. "Oh. I imagine he was in a lot of pain."

"He'll be back in action in no time. Probably be feeling better sooner than I will," Steve muttered under his breath. The feel of Jennifer's soft curves against him and knowing he could do nothing more than just hold her was sheer torture. But it was a torture he was willing to endure for at least a few more minutes even if it meant he'd pay for it with another restless night.

"What's the matter with you?"

"Er...ah...he smashed me up against the fence before we got him constrained. I'm going to be bruised down one side and probably feel it all over my body by tomorrow," he said, almost looking forward to that pain, hoping it would mask the aching in other parts of his anatomy he dared not tell her about.

"Poor baby," Jennifer murmured consolingly. "You should've stayed home and soaked in a hot tub." She snuggled a little closer, and Steve knew a cold shower would be of greater benefit.

She could hear the steady beat of his heart beneath her cheek. The rhythm was as hypnotizing as the soft strokes of his hands and the mesmerizing quality of his voice. She was so tired, and it felt so good to lean against his strength for just a little while. His closeness and touch were doing far more for her aches and pains than a couple of aspirin.

Yawning again, she asked sleepily, "How about the cat? Is he going to make it?"

He has a better chance than I have. Steve swallowed hard. Lord, he could use some of the anesthetic he'd administered to that damned bull today. "That wandering tom's going to be missing a few inches of his tail, have some dents and scars on his hips. He won't be as attractive to the ladies, but I think he'll be okay. We'll know more tomorrow."

Jennifer shifted her feet slightly and the action pushed her breasts more prominently against his chest. No, Steve decided, he couldn't stand this torture any longer. Bringing his hands back to her shoulders, he gently put some inches between them. "Go find a comfortable place to sit down, prop your feet up, and I'll warm up something for supper. Homemade vegetable beef soup, chicken and noodles, ham or meat loaf, your choice."

Still feeling somewhat dazed, Jennifer just stared at Steve. The menu choices he'd just rattled off made absolutely no sense.

Steve gulped again. Her eyes were limpid pools of dark gray. Her mouth looked moist, pink and way too inviting for his peace of mind. He'd set her away from him but not far enough. They were still too close to each other. Unable to ignore the softness of her mouth any longer, he lowered his head toward hers, moving slowly just in case she gave any sign of resistance. When none came, he brought his lips close enough to brush softly across hers.

Encouraged by the little shiver she gave just before leaning into him again, Steve settled his mouth more fully over hers.

It wasn't the kiss of one friend to another, and Jennifer knew she ought to end it before it intensified any further. But the scent and taste of him were sending such an energizing sizzle through her veins and along her nerves, and she couldn't resist the temptation to experience the sensation a little while longer.

Her arms wound naturally around his neck and just as naturally Steve's wrapped around her, pressing her more fully into the strength of his body. His mouth seared hers as his lips moved across them, his tongue soothing the burning sensation, then teasing her to open. She didn't fight the intrusion but welcomed it, feeling a fleeting second of regret that this embrace marked an end to any semblance of mere friendship between them. Then she gave herself up totally to the pleasures he was bestowing.

"Oh, Jennifer." Steve sighed, his lips leaving hers finally. Tipping her head against his chest so he couldn't look again into the eyes that had tempted him this far, he rested his cheek on top of her head. He drew a long, steadying breath and waited for his blood to cool enough so he could pull his arms away from her.

Not wanting to chance any comment on what had just happened between them, he effectively lightened the mood by asking, "What's your dining pleasure this evening, madam?" as soon as he'd put a safe distance between them.

Jennifer raised shaky hands to her hair, self-consciously smoothing it away from her face, though she wanted to lay her palms against her heated cheeks. Letting Steve Barthelmaus kiss her had definitely been a mistake, but in all honesty she had to admit to herself the kiss hadn't been remotely one-sided. "Er... ah... you choose," she stammered, grateful for the diversion. She couldn't have remembered any of the choices he'd rattled off earlier if her life had depended on it.

"It's Lisa's meat loaf, then," he told her, his grin dispelling the lingering heavy atmosphere. "That's her specialty, and it's even better than Mom's."

Once again Jennifer made a move toward a cupboard but once again Steve stopped her, though this time he was careful not to touch her. "Ah-ah-ah, get out of here. I'll cook—you are to be waited on. Marian's orders," he threw in for good measure against any show of resistance.

"Trust me, Jennifer. I'm an expert with a microwave. Being such a lousy cook, it's the only way I survive. Lucky for me, I've got Marian and I don't have to depend on commercially prepared frozen dinners. She comes twice a week to my house. One day to clean and do laundry. She grocery shops then cooks and bakes the other day until she's satisfied I've got enough meals to last till she can do it again."

Unable to resist, Jennifer asked, "What would you have done if I had let her stay with me?"

"Come here for supper every night, same as I'm doing right now," he told her as he opened the refrigerator. "Now get out of here so I can bumble around unobserved."

"I thought you said you were an expert."

"I lied."

"Maybe I'd better stay and help."

Steve glared over his shoulder at her, then cocked his head to one side. "Do I hear the baby crying?"

Jennifer listened, but heard nothing. She caught the mischievous grin on Steve's face. "Okay, I get the message. I'm out of here." She started toward her bedroom when a thought occurred to her. "Steve, would you mind listening for the baby?" Uncomfortable asking for another favor, but even more uncomfortable with her physical state, she stammered, "She shouldn't wake up for a little while longer... and I'd like to freshen up a bit, er...ah...take a shower, wash my hair."

"I'll listen for her. Take your time. Little babies are another thing I'm expert at."

"Why don't I feel assured?" Jennifer chided teasingly, fixing him with exaggerated narrow-eyed scrutiny.

The mischievous gleam disappeared from Steve's eyes. "Trust me, Jennifer. I've logged countless hours on my own with my nieces and nephews and haven't lost a one of them. Stephanie will be safe in my care."

Jennifer sobered as quickly as Steve. "I know, Steve," she said, wondering not for the first time what there was about this man that made her trust him so easily.

A shower in her own bathroom was heaven. Knowing Stephanie was fine under Steve's watchful eye, she lingered under the warm spray far longer than she would have chanced had she been alone.

By the time she turned off the spigots and wrapped herself in one of her own large fluffy towels, she was feeling like a new woman. So much so that she shunned donning another gown and robe, wanting instead to put on real clothes. Discarding one possibility after another as being too snug for her still-thickened waistline and wider hips, she finally settled on a pair of loose-fitting plum slacks with an elastic waist and a large one-size-fits-all cream-colored knit shirt. It was an outfit she'd bought when she'd first begun to expand but hadn't been large enough for maternity clothes.

Taking a look at herself in the full-length mirror on the back of her closet door, she turned sideways. Smoothing her hands over her abdomen, she decided she wasn't in too bad shape. She'd have some work to do in the coming weeks to get her figure back, but all in all, she was pretty pleased with the way she looked.

It was her own vanity that was appeased by her favorable assessment of herself, not a desire to impress the man who'd earlier kissed her so sweetly and thoroughly her toes had curled in pleasure. The kiss hadn't meant a thing! *He* certainly hadn't acted as if it had, so she wasn't going to read anything significant into it. Well, maybe one thing, she decided as she set to work on her hair.

It had been a masterful kiss. The logical conclusion was that Steve Barthelmaus was very experienced with them. "He's probably kissed hundreds of women," she said as she pushed her hair this way and that trying to decide what to do with it. "So many, kisses have become meaningless."

Catching up the hair on one side of her face, she rammed a comb into the mass to hold it in place and did the same on the other side. The pain of the plastic teeth scraping her scalp exceeded by only a little bit the pain she felt that the kiss she'd shared with Steve had been nothing to him.

"You are *not* going to care about this guy, Jennifer," she scolded as she applied blusher to her pale cheeks. She continued the lecture as she applied mauve color to her lips. If she never let herself care, she couldn't get hurt. It had taken her years to learn that lesson, and she wasn't about to unlearn it just because a gentle-touching, mesmerizing-voiced, honest-eyed, sweet-kissing veterinarian had managed to put a chink in her armor.

Sure that she'd strengthened her resolve to keep her relationship with Steve in its proper perspective, she shoved her feet into a pair of plum suede flats. Stephanie must be awake or about to awaken by now. Jennifer headed for the nursery.

The scene that greeted her there halted her in midstep. Steve was sitting in the rocking chair with Stephanie on his shoulder. A fresh diaper was draped over his shoulder and he was patting the baby's tiny back with the expertise of a pro. He looked so right that Jennifer felt a tiny lump grow in her throat. If only...

No! Fairy-tale endings were for little kids and maybe a few lucky people. She never had been nor ever would be one of those lucky people. She and Stephanie were a temporary interest to Steve. As long as she remembered that truth she could let herself enjoy his company and not be hurt when his fascination with the baby wore off.

Seemingly unaware that he was being observed, Steve was talking softly. "Come on, little girl. Big burp, this time. Forget the ladylike stuff. It's just you and me in here, so let it rip."

Stephanie obliged him with a something so loud it went beyond burp and right into champion belch. "All right!" Steve complimented at the same time Jennifer's giggle at the doorway made her presence known.

"What did you slip in her formula?" Jennifer asked as she moved into the room.

Waggling his eyebrows, Steve quipped, "Dr. Barthelmaus's secret." Settling the baby into the crook of his arm he directed his remarks to her. "Well Stephanie, you look too wide-eyed to go back to sleep. How'd you like to be the centerpiece for your mommy's and my dinner? You have to promise not to sing at the table, though." Turning to Jennifer, he asked, "Do you have one of those baby lounge chairs we can set in the middle of the table?"

Jennifer reached in the closet beside her. "This what you're talking about?" She held up an infant seat still wrapped in protective cellophane.

Steve grinned as he rose from the chair. "Your mommy thinks of everything. You're a lucky little girl." Looking at Jennifer, he let his gaze linger for a long moment. "She's pretty, too," he said with a wink as he passed her on the way out of the room.

Jennifer tried to ignore the satisfying warmth that spread through her body in reaction to his compliment. The comment had certainly been nothing more than a whim of the moment. His only real reason for taking such an interest in her plight was the inordinate responsibility he felt toward the baby he'd delivered, she reminded himself. "You really do know a lot about babies."

"The women in my family believe in equal opportunity," he stated as he strode briskly toward the dining room.

"Meaning?" Jennifer asked of the broad back she was following once again.

"Meaning, the men in the family have experienced every facet of baby and child care. And I mean every facet—including everything from changing diapers to cleaning up after a sick child," he added lest she not understand the extent of his knowledge.

Jennifer laughed at the disgruntled sound in his voice. "I think I'd like the women in your family."

Pausing by the table already set for their dinner, Steve waited for Jennifer to place the infant seat in the middle and adjust the back to its lowest setting. Carefully cradling Stephanie's head, he settled her into the seat and arranged a receiving blanket across her. Once he was sure she was secure, he turned to Jennifer with a grin, that sheepish little-boy grin that she was becoming more and more familiar with.

It was one that never failed to cause a quickening of her pulse. With a mother and two older sisters to practice it on, she suspected he'd been perfecting it all his life. Whether he knew it or not, and she suspected he did, it was guaranteed to soften even the hardest heart, for it certainly had that effect on her. Especially when accompanied by the warm-eyed look he was sending her right then.

Jennifer gulped and tried unsuccessfully to pull her gaze away from his.

"The feeling will be mutual," he said softly.

So preoccupied with his grin and eyes, Jennifer was too dazed to make any meaning of his comment. "What feeling?"

"My sisters and mother," he explained. "They're going to like you as much as I hope you'll like them."

"But I'll probably never meet—"

"Yes, you will," he informed her with infuriating confidence. Pulling a chair out for her, he ordered her to sit down. "We'll work out the details of your first meeting of the clan when you're feeling up to it."

Seven

"You and the baby go on into the living room, I'll clear up these dishes," Steve told Jennifer after they'd topped off their delicious meal with the chocolate chip cookies they hadn't had as a snack earlier.

Jennifer started to protest but Steve gave her a gentle shove toward the living room. "I came to serve you dinner, remember? That includes cleaning up afterward. Marian's orders."

Jennifer couldn't resist teasing, "She ordered you? I thought she worked for you."

"That's debatable," Steve quipped over his shoulder as he headed for the kitchen with a load of dishes. "When Mom and Dad retired from farming and moved to Arizona, Marian more or less adopted me. She seemed to think I was helpless to take care of myself, and she just showed up one day and took over."

"You and Mrs. Jenkins are two of a kind," Jennifer muttered under her breath as she settled herself and Stephanie on the sofa.

"What's that?" Steve called from the kitchen.

"Uh…Mrs. Jenkins is very kind," she called back.

Steve's response was muffled by the sound of running water.

Jennifer picked up the remote control resting on the coffee table, turned on the television and tuned in the evening news more from force of habit and to block out the sounds from the kitchen than from any real interest in what was happening in the world beyond her little house. The sweet-smelling perfect little life stretched out across her lap was all that was really important and made anything else inconsequential. She concentrated all her attention and efforts on coaxing a response from her newborn.

Clearing up the dinner dishes was a simple matter, Steve discovered. Less than ten minutes after he'd started, he was giving the kitchen a last look to make sure it would meet Marian's standards. Satisfied that he'd left it even better than he'd found it—another of the list of orders he'd been given—he pushed the button on the dishwasher and turned off the overhead light.

A glance at the kitchen clock told him it was still early. Even with the half hour drive back home, he'd still have plenty of hours left in the day to go over paperwork for either the clinic or the stable, check on his patients in the hospital ward, maybe give the kennel and the stables a last look over. Normally that's exactly what he would do, but tonight, attending to the day's paperwork seemed not only unimportant but a pretty dull way to spend the evening.

As for the hospital, kennels and stable, he had a well-trained staff to see to them. For once he didn't feel driven to oversee everything himself. He felt far more driven to spend time exactly where he was. What excuse he was going to use for lingering was his only problem.

Well, not the only problem, he realized as he started toward the living room and glimpsed Jennifer and the baby on the couch. Keeping his hands off that luscious woman was the bigger problem. Lord, what one kiss had done to his libido!

Though he felt drawn to that couch like a steel filing to a magnet, he forced himself to take a chair opposite Jennifer. "Anything important happening in the world?" he asked, noting the evening national news program was just finishing.

"Nobody declared war on us," Jennifer supplied, barely looking up when Steve entered. "At least I don't think so. We weren't paying much attention."

Steve picked up the newspaper and scanned the headlines. Surely there was something he could comment upon that might draw Jennifer into a conversation that would get his mind off kissing her again and give credence to his lingering. "The Reds won."

Busy brushing the baby's tiny fists against her lips, Jennifer murmured, "Mmm...that's nice."

"Looks like the Big Red Machine is really rolling again."

"That's my sweet girl.... Come on, move those little lips into a smile. I know you're pretty new at this but let's try for a smile," Jennifer continued, gurgling and playing with the baby.

"Some people are already betting they'll win the World Series again this year," he threw in absently, for lack of anything else to say.

"Too early. Better wait and see how they get through June," she managed to respond between nuzzling the baby's cheeks, fingers and toes.

"You know something about baseball?" Steve asked, not bothering to mask the incredulity in his voice.

"Just the Reds. I grew up in and around Cincinnati. Couldn't help learning something about baseball," she divulged between noisy caresses of the baby.

"Did you play ball when you were a kid?"

"Nothing organized, just with the other kids after school sometimes."

Sensing Jennifer's attention was so centered on the baby, she was barely aware of what she was saying, Steve kept up the conversation. This was the first she'd divulged anything about her background and he wanted to learn as much as he could before she threw up her walls.

"That's an advantage city kids often have over country kids. Playmates right next door. Are you from a big family?" he asked, keeping his tone nonchalant and his gaze on the newspaper opened in front of his face.

"No. I was my parents' only child," she said, her attention decidedly more on the baby than her words. "There were usually a lot of kids in the neighborhood, and then there were always at least six of us kids living in the house. If there were enough big ones we could get a pretty good game going."

Confused by her comments, Steve asked. "Did your parents raise a bunch of kids besides you?"

His question drew her full attention. Steve watched with apprehension as the radiance left her face.

"They . . . didn't even raise me," she stated in a flat tone.

Lifting the baby to her shoulder, she patted her tiny bottom. "This young lady needs a fresh diaper. Thanks for coming over and fixing dinner for me." She stood and yawned. The action was only slightly feigned.

"I think she and I need to retire early. We didn't sleep very well last night." Jennifer didn't try to keep the exhaustion from showing in her voice. She bit her lip to keep from telling him he knew where the door was and could let himself out, hoping instead that he'd take her less-than-subtle hint.

He was being dismissed again, as abruptly and firmly as she'd done it that first night at the hospital. Rising from his chair, Steve put a staying hand on Jennifer's shoulder as she attempted to step past him on her way to the nursery. Just as he'd done that first night, he willed her to look at him.

The wariness and vulnerability were in the deep gray depths of her eyes again, and Steve could almost feel the pain there, too. He'd opened a wound again. Maybe someday she'd let him close it for her. But not tonight. She wanted distance. He'd give her some, but not just yet.

Leaning down, he brushed his lips across the baby's head. "Good night, Stephanie." It was such a scant inch or so to Jennifer's lips that he took advantage and moved his own to hers. He allowed himself only a light press of his mouth to hers before moving his head away. "Get a good night's rest, Jennifer. I'll see you tomorrow."

"But that won't be necessary."

He could have mouthed the protest for her, so sure he'd been of her response. Smiling, he quipped, "Sure it is. Today was Marian's day to cook for me, but she cooked for you instead. I'll starve for sure if I don't come over here."

Turning on his heel, Steve was at the door shrugging into his coat before Jennifer could respond further. His hand on the doorknob, he turned back briefly. "Five-thirty, okay?"

"Do I have a choice?" Jennifer practically growled.

"Not really," he told her then whisked out the door.

Jennifer stared at the closed door for several minutes. "Stephanie, that is one very exasperating man! What are we going to do about him?"

True to his word—or *threat* to Jennifer's way of thinking—Steve showed up the next evening and prepared dinner for her. Though she told him once again at the end of the evening that he didn't need to come back the next day, he ignored her and continued to show up nightly.

It was difficult for her to admit, but at the end of each day she actually looked forward to the company of another adult, as well as the pampering he insisted upon showering on her. He arrived promptly at five-thirty each evening, prepared, served and then cleared up their dinner as well as any other dishes that had accumulated during the day. Afterward he lingered, watched the evening news, sometimes read her newspaper. Once he even ran the vacuum through the house, overriding her protests by claiming he was under orders from Marian. And always he found an excuse to hold and play with the baby. Each evening the length of his stay stretched out a little bit longer.

The days gradually settled into a pattern. Though it would be weeks before the baby could be expected to start sleeping through the night, Stephanie did settle into a reasonable nighttime routine of awaking only every three to four hours for a feeding and taking a nice long nap every afternoon. Jennifer took advantage and rested, too. Only rarely did Jennifer find herself pacing the floor with a fussy baby during the midnight hours.

Though she longed for eight uninterrupted hours of sleep as she faced each new day through bleary eyes, Jennifer began to feel her strength return. However, her emotions still seemed too close to the surface for her peace of mind, and Steve's continued evening visits weren't helping. Sure that she couldn't handle any more of his skillful kisses or intoxicating embraces, she tried for both a physical and emotional distance between herself and Steve each evening.

Her attempts were in vain.

Physical distance was impossible, no matter how hard she tried to avoid being within arm's length of the man. He was a toucher and always found ways to rest his hand on her shoulder, brush it over the top of her head, slip his arm around her waist. These gestures could have been interpreted as innocent touches, despite the way her own pulse rate accelerated each time and the way his eyes darkened. Though she always moved away from his touch, it gradually became more and more difficult for Jennifer to force herself to do so.

And then there were the good-night kisses.... Never again as fiery or lengthy as the first time he'd kissed her, but only because Jennifer summoned a resistance from deep down in her soul and pushed out of his arms before the kiss could escalate. Though her good sense told her she should avoid these kisses altogether, she somehow never quite managed that and allowed herself to be folded into his arms every night.

Physical distance wasn't the only losing battle she fought. The emotional distance she thought she wanted kept growing shorter and shorter. The man's continued presence made it impossible, for she was getting to know him too well. He told her about his day with his animal patients and drew her out to tell him about her day with Stephanie. He shared his dream of establishing a Standardbred stud and the hopes he was pinning on the two harness racers he and his father co-owned.

And always there were the stories about his family, strengthening Jennifer's conviction that she'd like them all. At the same time she steeled herself against becoming so enthralled by them that her imagination might run with the image of herself and Stephanie in their midst. Neither the opportunity nor the reason would ever arise that she would even meet them. She'd make sure of it. What she didn't know, she couldn't miss. She was already going to miss Steve a lot when he got over his feelings of responsibility toward her and Stephanie. She didn't want to miss his family, too.

Usually it was during mealtimes that Steve regaled her with family stories. She tried to listen with only half an ear and attempted to commit nothing to memory. That proved impossible as Steve was an excellent storyteller, painting vivid pictures with humorous anecdotes as he introduced her to each family member.

By the time they'd gone through all of Lisa's meat loaf, her vegetable soup, two jars of jam—made from strawberries that had been set out by his grandmother and prepared by his mother when she and his father made their last summer trip to Ohio—Karen's chocolate chip cookies and chicken casserole, and had started into the second week's offerings of equally delicious family specialties, Jennifer felt she would recognize every Barthelmaus at first sight, even some of their pets.

She wanted to scream in frustration. She didn't want to yearn to meet these people. She didn't want to know there was a family living just inside the next county that fit every dream of one she'd ever had. Though she hadn't been able to keep from laughing at some of Steve's stories or make a comment on others, after close to two weeks of this, she was so close to tears she couldn't utter a sound by the end of this evening's session.

Her increasing reticence and the stricken look on her face didn't go unnoticed. Steve reached across the table and squeezed her hand. "Tired?"

Jennifer nodded her head. She wasn't, really. Most of her normal stamina was back, but she was glad for the excuse he'd given her. "Sorry. I'm not a very good hostess this evening," she got out over the lump in her throat.

"You're the perfect hostess," Steve corrected with another of his engaging grins. His hand remained over hers, lightly stroking it as he talked. "You always let your guest do all the talking. It's long past being your turn."

"My turn?" she asked dumbly.

"To bore me to death. For at least the next week, you may totally dominate all conversations with stories about your family and I promise to nod and smile at the appropriate times just like you did."

Jennifer slid her hand away from his stroking fingers and used it to push her chair away from the table. "I won't need a week, not even an hour." Stacking their plates and silverware, she began clearing the table. "My mother died when I was very young and my father—"

Squeezing her eyes shut, she leaned on the table for a moment waiting for the anger to subside. "He's dead now, too."

Her hesitation piqued his curiosity, but he knew if he queried her, she'd close up like a clam. Little by little the pieces that made up the puzzle that was Jennifer Lewis were falling together.

Though he'd like to pull her into his arms, he merely placed his hands on her shoulders. "I'm sorry, Jennifer."

Shrugging away from his consoling touch, Jennifer pasted a shaky smile on her face. "Thanks, but it all happened a long time ago. I grew up in foster homes."

Her remark explained some of the mystery created by her statement of over a week ago. Steve knew it didn't take a genius to figure out that her foster home upbringing had been painful for her. Where had her father been?

Like a lightning bolt, her near-hysterical ramblings that first night at the hospital came back to him. Her comments about the child-welfare department, nobody taking her baby away from her, not being helpless and more had been chilling then, and were more so now. He didn't know the reason why it had happened, but it was clear that Jennifer had been taken away from her father.

Wishing he could sweep her up in his arms and soothe away the pain she was trying so hard to disguise, he offered, "That must have been rough," knowing how very inadequate his words were.

"I got used to not having a family of my own," she said, her tone almost flippant, so much so that Steve knew it was another cover.

Carefully she lifted the baby up from the infant seat and cradled her warm little body close. "But now I've got Stephanie and we're a family."

Not quite, Steve thought to himself. There's a lot missing in this picture, especially one very important member, and the man's an idiot! Unconsciously, his body stiffened and his hands curled into fists.

Knowing now how truly alone in the world she was and all she'd suffered, he was even more inflamed at the man who'd deserted her. A man who could skip out on the woman carrying his child didn't deserve to call himself a man. He was just beginning to know Jennifer, but if there was one thing he was sure about with this woman it was that she wasn't the type to give her heart easily. Hell, just wrangling her permission to be her friend had been difficult.

That incredible kiss they'd shared a couple of weeks ago notwithstanding, he would also bet his new operating room that the way she'd been holding herself aloof ever since indicated she didn't give her body any more easily than she gave her heart. Some smooth-talking jerk had sure led her down the primrose path, taken his pleasure, then skipped out when responsibility reared its head. No wonder she was so hell-bent on keeping him at arm's length. If he ever got his hands on that man, he'd pound him to pulp!

"Something wrong?" Jennifer asked, startled by Steve's black expression. Taking in his clenched fists and bristling body, she took a wary step back.

"There most certainly is," Steve blurted. From the first she'd aroused protective instincts in him. With each passing day he'd felt his animosity grow toward the man who'd deserted Jennifer. Tonight all that animosity erupted.

In a stream of vitriolic condemnations, he told her exactly what he thought of Stephanie's sire and exactly what he thought should be done to the man. "How could you have let yourself get involved with such an irresponsible bastard!"

Jennifer couldn't believe she was hearing this kind of language from the gentle, caring man who'd been keeping her company each evening. What's more, his accusation, however off-base it was, stung. Hurriedly she moved several more steps away from him, thankful the baby was too young to comprehend the words that had just been bellowed. However, Stephanie wasn't too young not to react to the heightened volume and vehemence of Steve's speech and soon her bellows were matching Steve's.

"Now look what you've done!" Jennifer yelled angrily then went about soothing her child. She started for the nursery, her glare telling Steve he'd better not follow.

Away from that suddenly hateful man, she still needed several minutes to calm the baby, especially since she herself needed calming. It was easy to guess the conclusions Steve had drawn, and she couldn't really blame him. Though the details of Stephanie's conception weren't something she'd felt would ever be necessary to explain to him, Jennifer knew it would be a mistake not to do so now. A week ago she might well have used his misunderstanding of the situation as an excuse to see the last of him. But now that had all changed.

She didn't exactly know where their relationship was going, wasn't even sure she wanted it to go anywhere, but she did know she needed to clear this matter up with the truth. She really couldn't let him continue to think what he was obviously thinking. She didn't want his pity and she most definitely didn't want his condemnation. It would be far easier to assume he thought well of her when he moved on to other interests.

Once the baby was settled and sleeping peacefully in her bassinet, and she felt composed, Jennifer sought Steve out.

He wasn't hard to find. Her house wasn't large but the level of crashing and clanking in the kitchen would have led her to him if the house had been a twin to Buckingham Palace. Coming to a stop just inside the kitchen entry, she asked, "Have I any plates left?"

Steve dropped one more plate into the dishwasher then slammed the door closed. His temper was still running high, but better leashed. "Enough. I'm sorry I scared the baby. Believe me, I'd never do anything to hurt that precious little girl."

Jennifer nodded. However, there was an unspoken *but* dangling at the end of his last statement. She waited for him to continue. When several long moments dragged by and he remained silent, she prompted, "But...?"

Steve wadded up the dish towel he'd been worrying in his hands and threw it at a corner of the counter. "Dammit, Jennifer. I look at you and that beautiful baby and I get furious with the man who deserted you."

"He didn't desert me. He wasn't expected to be responsible."

Her quietly spoken statements had a sledgehammer effect on Steve. Feeling as if he'd just had all the air knocked out of him, he just stood staring open-mouthed at her.

Jennifer used his silence to prepare her explanation. Before she'd gone through with the procedure, she'd read everything she could about donor insemination. The information always included the husband's reactions since in most cases of D.I. the choice was made by a married couple wherein the husband was infertile. The feelings of inadequacy and even jealousy toward the unknown donor that husbands frequently experienced shouldn't apply to Steve, but as an attorney, she knew better than to assume anything. She also knew that there would be some men who would assume she was a man hater for choosing to have a baby without the direct services of a man. How Steve reacted to the truth she was about to divulge was going to tell her a great deal about his character.

"I think we'd better go into the living room and sit down," she began, almost enjoying having completely flummoxed Dr. Know-What's-Best-Take-Over Barthelmaus. He was usually so sure of himself. It felt good to shatter him a bit. "By the looks of you, this is going to take a little explaining."

"Damned right it is," Steve remarked as he strode toward the living room, trying hard to come to grips with the glaring proof that he'd completely misjudged this woman's character. Perversely he felt betrayed and that really goaded him. "What are you going to tell me? That you hired a stud?"

Stifling the impulse to give him the put-down he deserved for his crude remark, Jennifer lowered herself gracefully to the couch. Folding her shaking hands neatly in her lap, she schooled her features to appear serene. "Stephanie was conceived via artificial insemination. I assume you are familiar with the procedure?"

"Artificial insemination...?" The information was startling, but it had the immediate effect of pouring oil on rough waters. He could almost feel his blood pressure dropping. The wind effectively knocked out of his sails, he crossed his legs and cleared his throat.

"Well of course I'm familiar with the procedure. It's quite common in animal breeding." Embarrassment and self-condemnation for what he'd said earlier washed over him, and the control he'd gained slipped. Running a nervous hand through his hair he admitted, "I've spent these past weeks all but taking out a contract on a guy who doesn't even exist and then accuse you of— I'm sorry."

"You didn't know. It was an understandable mistake."

"Hardly!" He scoffed. "I was acting like a damned fool and you know it. I'm supposed to be a man of science, someone who gathers all the information before making a diagnosis." Feeling chagrined, he ran his hands down his jaws, then repeated more to himself than to Jennifer, "Artificial insemination. I'll be damned."

"In humans, the procedure's usually called donor insemination," she told him, uneasy with his reaction so far but driven to continue with the discussion. "How do you feel about it?"

He started to tell her he didn't think it sounded like much fun and he'd rather use the old-fashioned method of getting a baby, but immediately rejected the thought. "Obviously I'm more familiar with its application in animals, but I know enough about its use with humans to know that it's an option in a variety of cases. I assume you had a really good reason for choosing D.I., and it's probably none of my business, which I'm sure you're going to point out, but would you mind sharing your reason with me?"

She'd gone this far, so she steeled herself to reveal the rest. She curled her legs up beside her on the couch and clasped her hands tightly. "Possible infertility," she said simply. She chanced a glance at Steve's face and knew her answer wasn't enough to satisfy him. Talking about her body to any other man would have been impossible, but she admitted to herself Steve was like no other man.

As succinctly as possible, she explained her physician's discovery of ovarian cysts, the surgery she'd gone through two years before, and that it had resulted in the removal of one of her ovaries. "Since the probability of reoccurrence of ovarian cysts is quite high, Dr. Canfield suggested I get pregnant almost immediately if I wanted to have a child. Having only one ovary and being past thirty decreased my fertility odds."

"And so you chose donor insemination," Steve filled in for her. He closed the space between them and slipped his arm around her shoulders. The explanation hadn't been easy for her, he knew. Maybe a reassuring arm, a hug, would ease the tension he saw in her face. He felt the stiffness of her body.

"I wanted a child of my own very badly and I didn't have any other options," she said, confirming the high opinion he had formed about her before he'd started thinking so irrationally.

Finding out that there was no man to turn up and claim her and the baby was such a relief Steve wanted to shout for joy. He'd been feeling as though he'd been trespassing on somebody else's territory and now he knew the coast was clear for him.

To do what? he paused to ask himself. He had his answer in less than a second. It came to him with the unexpected suddenness of a sunbeam dropping through a dark cloud: claim her as his own.

That's what he'd like to do and in the most primal way, but he knew the slightest move in that direction would scare her off for sure. Sharing the details of Stephanie's conception was another major breakthrough in Jennifer's learning to trust him. He'd have to be careful not to lose the precious ground he'd gained.

Stifling a desire to sweep her into his arms and let her know just how much he wanted to claim her, he satisfied himself by snuggling her just a little closer and pressing her head to his shoulder. Her lack of resistance was like a gift.

"For what it's worth, I want you to know I respect your decision," he began, praying he'd say the right words and all the while wishing he could say what he really thought. *If you'd waited a few more months, you would definitely have had another option—me!* "Thanks for sharing with me how you got Stephanie. Considering what a jerk I was a while ago, I'm surprised you didn't throw me out."

"Don't think I didn't consider it," she grumbled, though her irritation was false.

"You really had me going there for a while, didn't you?"

"Served you right."

They sat on the couch, side by side, in companionable silence for several minutes. When Jennifer yawned, Steve suggested, "I think I'd better go before you fall asleep on me."

"That's probably a good idea," Jennifer said on another yawn, but made no move toward lifting her head away from his shoulder. Though she was almost completely recovered physically from Stephanie's birth, she found she tired earlier in the evening than usual. Tonight had been particularly draining. Resting against Steve's warm strong body for just another moment or two would give her the strength to walk him to the door, turn out the lights and seek her own bed.

Steve winced inwardly when she snuggled a bit closer. "Jennifer...?"

When she turned her head and looked up at him, he was lost. Her eyes were soft and slumberous. Her lips were moist and pink. And her body felt so soft and wondrously feminine.

Folding her closer, he captured her mouth beneath his. He started the kiss gently, knowing any sign of the fierce possessiveness he was feeling toward her would frighten her. He traced his tongue along the fullness of her lips, tasting, soothing and coaxing.

Sensing a reluctance in her at first, he patiently persisted until at last his wooing was successful. Pressing his tongue snugly in her mouth, he felt her tremble. Or maybe it was his own trembling, for he'd certainly never felt this way before when he'd been merely holding and kissing a woman.

A tremor ran through his body. His breathing became more labored as he fought against the raging impulses coursing through his body. Jennifer was fragile, both physically and emotionally. He needed to control his primitive needs. His good intentions were nearly lost when she moaned softly and arched against him.

No matter what Jennifer had been telling herself about keeping an emotional distance from this man, she wanted this kiss, needed it as an affirmation that she was desirable. It had been such a long time since she'd felt anything like this toward a man. Years, really. Not since a brief affair during law school had she let a man get close enough for anything more than a perfunctory good-night kiss. It was so much safer that way.

Allowing her relationship with Steve to escalate beyond friendship wasn't playing it safe. But right then she didn't care about safeguarding her emotions. She could throw up her guards another time. For now her instincts told her she could trust him and give herself up to the glory to be found in his arms.

His mouth was tender as his lips taught her new sensations. When he shifted their positions on the couch and bore her down beneath him, she welcomed the weight of his body. When she felt the heels of his hands brush against the sides of her breasts, she wanted him to soothe their aching. Squirming beneath him to provide better access, she was only partly gratified when he lightly palmed their fullness and stroked his thumbs across their peaks.

Groaning again, Steve lifted his mouth from hers on a tortured breath. Resting his forehead against hers, he choked out, "No more. You're not ready for anything else."

Trembling with frustration and embarrassment, Jennifer struggled to bring her breathing under control. Blushing furiously, she mumbled, "I'm sorry."

"Not your fault," he said against her smooth brow. "I'm the one who started it. I'm rushing you and I'm the one to be apologizing. For that and being such a jerk earlier."

Pressing a quick kiss to her forehead, he lifted his body away from hers. "I'm definitely going now." Standing quickly before he changed his mind, he held his hand out to her. "Walk me to the door?"

Jennifer sensed he was reaching out to offer more than just help up from the couch. After a moment's hesitation, she met the smile and the hand which was offered.

At the door he slipped on the lightweight jacket he'd hung on the coat rack, then pulled her into a light embrace. "I meant what I said before. I do respect your decision to have Stephanie the way you did."

"Thank you," she said, relieved that telling him hadn't been a mistake.

His mouth curved into an irresistible smile. "If you hadn't, we might never have gotten to know each other, and that, pretty lady, would have been a tragedy."

"You think so?"

"I know so." He swept her up against him, and in a kiss far from his usual chaste farewells he confirmed again that friendship was not at all what he was seeking from her any longer.

Eight

"**H**ey, little brother," Karen Kegan greeted, her large brown eyes dancing with humor. Right beside her was Steve's other sister, Lisa Fruth, her eyes, blue like her brother's, glinting with the same humor as Karen's.

Looking at the two of them leaning against the counter in his clinic's waiting room, Steve didn't need a crystal ball to tell him what they were there for. The only mystery was what had taken them so long.

"Good afternoon, big sisters. Where are your kids?" he returned, knowing their answer would provide only a brief reprieve from the inquisition he was about to be put through.

"Marian's stuffing the little ones with cookies and milk up at the house. The big kids headed for the practice track the minute they spied your new trainer. Don Miller is it?" Lisa paused just long enough for Steve to nod confirmation. "As soon as they saw him out there working Mr. Bart they were sprinting toward the fence.''

"I hear Mr. Bart's been winning or placing in every race so far and Sorrel Blazer's been establishing a pretty respectable name for herself, too," Karen chipped in, her voice overly nonchalant. "Of course we heard that long-distance from Dad...."

"Dad was so excited about the horses' times and wins, he called us all the way from Arizona. Sure was nice of your trainer to let Dad know how the horses were doing, since his partner seems so occupied otherwise," Lisa said, but the wicked gleam in her eyes belied the casual tone in her speech.

Both sisters turned to their brother with raised eyebrows. Steve threw his hands up in defeat. "All right, you two. What is it you really want to know?" he asked, not impressed with their attempt at diversion.

Though his sisters liked horses, could each handle the ribbons on a racing sulky with acceptable expertise, neither particularly cared about a horse's time around the track. As long as a horse had pretty markings and had a friendly gentle temperament, they were satisfied. A friendly gentle nature being common in Standardbreds, both Bart and Blaze were favorites of theirs.

It was Karen, the middle child, the biggest tease, but the Barthelmaus offspring with the greatest sense of honor and justice who supplied the answer. "Jennifer Lewis. The Fourth of July in a few days. You are going to bring her to the celebration aren't you? Seems like the perfect time for us to finally meet this wonder woman who's got our little brother's heart in her hands.''

Color rose from Steve's neck to his cheeks. He could feel it. Clearing his throat, he fiddled around with the pens stuck in a mug on the counter. "Just what makes you think I'm in love with her?" he asked, surprised how right it felt to use the word love in connection with Jennifer. For weeks he'd been skirting around that possibility in his own mind. However, he wasn't about to announce his thoughts to his sisters.

Despite the way the goodbyes he shared with Jennifer each evening were becoming more and more prolonged and the way she finally let herself melt against him and give as much as he gave, the time was far from ripe for any declarations. There was still a wariness about her each time he arrived and a definite reluctance on her part to discuss what was happening between them.

"How do we know he loves her? Let us count the ways," Lisa parodied. "For starters you've hot-footed out of this clinic on the heels of your last patient every day since you met her."

"Not every day," Steve defended, though in fact he did wish it were every day. Now that Jennifer was truly back on her feet, she'd allowed him only every other evening at best. "Besides, haven't you both been telling me I spend too much after-hours time here? And just how do you know I've been leaving right after patients some evenings?"

"Aha, he admits it," Karen announced in triumph, receiving a burning glare from Steve. "Okay, so your receptionist told Marian and she told us."

Before Steve could respond to that information, Lisa launched another volley. "You have yet to attend a race that either of your horses have been entered in this season."

"That's not true. I watched Blaze when she raced at Scioto Downs. They've been racing mostly out of state. I do have a practice to run back here. I can't hang out at the tracks all the time."

"Never stopped you before," Karen reminded him. "When the harness-racing season began, you were gone more than you were here."

"That's not true. I only went to the out-of-state weekend races."

"And all the ones in state plus checking the competition at Scioto Downs even when you didn't have one of your own horses entered," Lisa added then went on relentlessly. "Just how have you been spending all your after-hours time this summer, hmm?"

"Don's a good horseman," Steve stated evasively. "Dad and I trust him implicitly. He knows what he's doing. I don't have to hover around the track or the stables checking up on him."

"Oh sure. The other guy is so bad the Overmeyer Stables snatched him up after the Little Brown Jug last year," Karen quipped.

"Okay, okay. I just felt that Jennifer and the baby needed me more than Don did. She doesn't have any family around and needs somebody to take care of her."

"For this long?" Lisa's eyes were glittering with laughter. "She didn't need anybody after the first week. The truth is you can't stand to spend one evening away from her, and that's a real first for you."

Karen came around the counter and draped an arm on Steve's shoulder, patting him consolingly. "It's okay, Stevie. When the love bug bites, it bites hard, and you, my dear, have most assuredly been bitten. Haven't we all always said you'd fall someday, and

when you did you'd fall hard? It's definitely time we
met Jennifer and got our hands on the miracle baby
you helped deliver."

"Yeah," Lisa agreed. "We'll even make it easy on
you. We'll bring all the food. All you have to do is
provide the guest of honor and plenty of charcoal for
the grill. Come on, Stevie," she coaxed. "It'll give us
a chance to look her over and give our stamp of ap-
proval. It's a tradition, remember?"

Steve looked from one sister to the other as he pon-
dered the wisdom of subjecting an unsuspecting Jennifer to the entire clan. Over the years he'd brought an
assortment of females to family picnics, especially the
bash they threw every Fourth of July. High school and
college girlfriends, and later occasionally a woman
he'd been seeing, but nobody recently. He knew exactly what would happen if he invited Jennifer and the
baby, especially the tradition part.

There could be the usual jesting about Jennifer
being the latest G.O.Y., Girl of the Year. Thank
goodness his father wouldn't be there or he'd start the
betting on the odds of this G.O.Y. becoming a per-
manent addition to the clan. He wouldn't put it past
either of his sisters' husbands to carry on the tradition in their father-in-law's absence. The girls who'd
overheard this teasing had rolled with it and taken it
in the spirit it had been delivered. But those times were
different. Jennifer was different. He didn't want to
take a chance of her being scared off. What was
building between them was too new, too fragile and
far too important to put at risk.

A jab in the ribs brought him out of his contempla-
tion. "Lisa, I do believe Stevie doesn't trust us."

"We'll behave, Steven." Lisa pulled a serious face, straightened her spine and held up her hand in a three-fingered salute. "Scout's honor."

"No. G.O.Y. stuff and no betting," Steve stated, his expression and tone serious enough to sober his sisters and gain their promises as well as assurances they'd warn their husbands against the same.

Lisa leaned over the counter and planted a kiss on her brother's cheek. "Jennifer's really special, isn't she?"

"Yes, she really is," Steve admitted with a dreamy expression. He knew it told his sisters as clearly as if he'd said the words that his thoughts were centered on the future. It was a look they hadn't seen in his eyes for a good three years, not since the day a prancing Standardbred yearling, who would become Mr. Bart, had been delivered to the farm. Before that, they'd seen it when he'd outlined his plans for the clinic and kennels he would build when he graduated from vet school.

Before that? Maybe when he'd revealed who his date was for the junior prom. Despite all their, and a good percentage of the county's matchmaking attempts, no girl or woman had quite captured his full attention until Jennifer Lewis. He'd never lacked for dates. Some girls, and later a handful of young women, had even lasted several months. But never had he been so worried about the impression his family might make or how they might behave. This was definitely serious.

After convincing his sisters he'd do his best to meet them at the usual corner on Main Street for the Independence Day parade, they left to collect their broods. Despite the optimistic assurances he'd given them, he

knew he was going to have to do some fast talking to
get Jennifer to agree to the all-day affair. Every weekend he'd tried to pry her out of her house to spend at
least an afternoon in the country. Always the answer
was no, not outright, but the meaning of her evasive
measures was the same.

At first she'd said she wasn't quite up to any out-
ings, and he'd respected that. Then she'd used the
baby's size and age as reasons why she didn't want to
take her out quite yet. He'd bowed to that excuse also,
chalking it up to first-time mother overprotective-
ness.

Neither excuse washed any longer, as Jennifer was
so well recovered. She'd driven the baby to her first-
month pediatric appointment herself, gone grocery
shopping and dropped in at the law firm with the
baby. She'd started doing some work at home and in-
terviewed possible nannies in preparation for the time
she'd be back in her office full-time.

The baby was growing like the proverbial weed,
putting on weight so satisfactorily she wasn't far behind full-term babies her age. Stephanie could not be
used as an excuse anymore. There was something else,
something that had no real basis but was still very real
to Jennifer. The last couple of weekends the look in
her eyes, when she'd manufactured some reason to
turn down his invitation, had been close to fear, as if
visiting his home truly frightened her.

"What are you scared of, Jennifer?" he asked aloud
to the empty room. He stood, shrugged out of his lab
jacket and hung it up. Delaware County was predom-
inantly country compared to its neighbor, Franklin, to
the south where metropolitan Columbus dominated.
However, as country as Delaware County might be it

wasn't the jungle. There was absolutely nothing dangerous to be found in the gentle rolling hills and farmlands that made up the area.

He continued to ponder what there was about coming to his place that alarmed Jennifer, while he trudged up the winding brick path between the clinic and his house and throughout the time it took him to shower and change clothes. During the drive to Jennifer's in Columbus, he mulled over several possible answers. Distance? Twenty-five minutes from her house to his. It took about that long to get from her house in the northwest section of the city to the parking lot of her office building in the center of the city.

No plausible answer was forthcoming, and when Jennifer opened her door, his expression must have revealed some of his bewilderment for she immediately asked, "Something wrong?"

"No, just a long day," he lied as he started through the entryway.

Reaching out, Jennifer caught Steve's forearm, effectively stopping his progress. The feel of the hair-covered muscular arm exposed by his short-sleeved polo shirt immediately sent a shaft of desire straight through her. Quickly she withdrew her hand.

"You should turn around and go straight home," she ordered, knowing it was the opposite of what she craved. She was coming to rely far too much on his company, to look forward too much to their embraces, and daydreaming too much about what could be. Most of all, she was spending far too many nights thinking her bed was way too large for only one person.

"You're running yourself ragged coming into the city so many times a week and for what?" she asked, trying not to let the annoyance she felt with herself show in her tone. "I'm fully recovered now and perfectly capable of taking care of myself and Stephanie. Dinner's almost ready to come out of the oven. I fixed it myself, exactly as I've been doing for quite some time. Unlike some people I could name, I'm not likely to starve if I'm left on my own. Go home, Steve. Your evenings would be better spent taking care of yourself."

Steve's first impulse was to turn on his heel and march right back through the door. But he hesitated. The moment was long enough for him to catch something in her eyes. Something about the way she couldn't quite meet his gaze prompted him to ask her the question he'd been asking since his sisters had left him alone at the clinic. "What are you afraid of, Jennifer?"

The softly spoken question brought Jennifer's gaze to Steve's face. It was a mistake to let her eyes be drawn directly to his, for once caught there, she couldn't pull her gaze away. The warmth emanating from the soft blue depths had as disconcerting an effect on her right then as it had the very first time.

A soft sound, half moan half sigh escaped her throat. *I'm afraid of you! Myself! Most of all the disappointment and heartache I'm going to suffer when you tell me you're moving on to someone else.* That was the honest answer to his question, but Jennifer didn't have the courage to say the words aloud. Instead she lifted her chin slightly and hedged with "I don't know what you mean."

Steve took a step closer, then another until he had her trapped in a corner, literally with his body and figuratively with what he was demanding of her. "Let me rephrase that," he began with his usual smooth and easy tone, but his eyes had kindled in a way that made her knees weak. "Do you honestly believe that I've been coming here all these weeks for no other reason than to help you out?"

Both drawn and frightened by the look he was giving her, Jennifer nervously licked lips suddenly gone dry. "I...I can't know what's going on in your head," she said, unwilling to put a name to his motivations lest she be wrong.

Cradling her face in his hands, the blue of his eyes darker than she'd ever seen it, he brushed his mouth lightly across hers. "Maybe this will help," he murmured before settling his mouth more firmly over hers.

He kissed her slowly, deeply and possessively. His mouth wasn't hard, his tongue not rough, yet she sensed a new fierceness in him that hadn't been there before. The feelings he was arousing in her were frightening in their intensity and she whimpered softly.

She tried to draw away but Steve wasn't allowing any escape. He plunged his hands into her hair and captured her head firmly, anchoring her exactly where he wanted her while his mouth and tongue did exquisitely arousing things to hers. The taste, texture and heat of his kiss overcame her fears and she sank into him, her body suddenly gone warm and fluid.

Finally, when Jennifer was sure she couldn't bear any more of this exquisite torture, he relaxed his hold on her head. Still cupping her face between his palms, he brushed his lips across her eyelids, then skimmed them down her cheeks. "I care for you, Jennifer, a lot. At first I came because I believed you needed caring for. Now I come because I want to and need to.

Spending my evenings with you and Stephanie is taking care of *myself*."

Still shaken by the intensity of the kiss, all Jennifer could manage as a response was to form a small circle with her mouth and a sound came out in the semblance of a breathless "Oh."

Taking advantage, Steve dipped his head again and began anew the assault on her senses that he'd wrought only seconds before. Somewhere deep in the recesses of Jennifer's mind, warning bells were ringing, but she ignored them and gloried in the feel of his lips and tongue taking hers with such possession. When he dropped his hands from her cheeks, swept his arms around her and aligned her with the hard contours of his body, the bells sounded louder.

She was enjoying this kiss and everything else about Steve too much. Stiffening, she moved her arms from around his neck and with every ounce of willpower she could conjure tore her mouth from his and mumbled the only excuse she could think of. "Dinner."

"Mmm...smells good," he said against her cheek.

Putting a little distance between them, Jennifer shook her head slightly to clear her brain. "It's baked chicken," she managed to add, having brought herself partway back to the world of the coherent. Giving Steve a little shove, she took advantage of his loosened hold and escaped the corner on unsteady legs. "You did bring dessert, didn't you?"

"Dessert...?" Steve took several deep breaths before he understood what she was asking. "Dessert," he repeated before realization dawned on him. "Damn. I knew there was something I was supposed to remember. My sisters stopped by just as I was about to leave and well..."

He paused, wondering if now wasn't the best time
to bring up the annual Independence Day celebration. Later when his wits were with him, he decided,
and rambled on with an excuse about their visit caus-
ing him to run late and not think about anything but
the time. "How does a trip to that new ice-cream place
on Lane Avenue sound?"

"Fattening," Jennifer returned over her shoulder as
she headed toward the kitchen.

"I'll carry the baby and we'll walk. That ought to
burn off the calories," he suggested, though watching Jennifer's retreat, he didn't think she needed to
worry about calories.

She was wearing a pair of white cotton knit pants
that skimmed across her hips perfectly. The fabric
clung relentlessly and unforgivingly across the smooth
lines of her body. If there had been any excess inches
on her, they most definitely would have been revealed. And he knew for a fact that her cable-stitched
cotton sweater wasn't hiding a thick waistline. He'd
spanned his hands around that waist enough times in
the past weeks to guess that it was back to its prepreg-
nancy size. He had no way of knowing what kind of
figure she'd had before, but the one she had now had
been keeping him awake at night. After the kiss they'd
just had, he knew he was condemned to another
sleepless night.

A happy gurgling sound from the vicinity of the
living room detoured his thoughts from the path
they'd been taking. Always glad for the chance to pick
up the baby and play with her a bit, he was happier
than usual to turn his attention solely on Stephanie.
Another moment or two of his speculating over how
good Jennifer's body would look clad in absolutely

nothing and he'd need a cold shower before he could get through dinner.

"Hello, little lady," Steve greeted as he crouched down beside the quilt Jennifer had spread on the floor. In reaction to his voice, Stephanie kicked her feet and favored him with what he could swear was a smile, a little lopsided but a smile just the same. "Thatta girl, Sunshine," he crooned, delighted with her obvious recognition of him.

Scooping her up, he nestled her securely in the crook of his arm and settled himself in the comfortable wide-armed chair nearby. Until Jennifer called him to dinner a few minutes later, Steve "chatted" with the baby, charming more smiles and cooing noises from her to the delight of both of them.

He was no less charming during the meal he shared with the baby's mother, coaxing smiles and conversation from her almost as easily as he had from the baby.

Though he made no mention of the declaration he'd given upon his arrival, Jennifer noticed there was a subtle shift in his behavior toward her. Frequently she looked up to discover his eyes on her, steady and compelling, seemingly willing an answer from her to an unspoken query. She knew he wanted, deserved, some sort of like declaration from her and was giving her this time to marshal her thoughts.

By the meal's end, Jennifer's nerves were leaping at the sound of his voice, and her heart was skipping a beat every time her gaze met his. Needing to calm her nerves and desperate for a change in scenery, she was grateful for his suggestion to walk to a newly opened ice-cream shop for dessert.

"How'd you know about this place?" Jennifer asked as she moved past the door Steve held open for her. The independent establishment specialized in ice cream made on the premises, strictly a Ma and Pa outfit from what she'd read in the promotion material published in the local suburban newspaper.

"We Delaware Countians get around," he supplied with a grin, his blue eyes twinkling.

Having relaxed considerably along the way, Jennifer was able to go along with his light mood. Rolling her eyes, she let out a short snort that let him know how little credence she put in his explanation.

"A high school classmate of mine and her husband are the owners," Steve supplied. "Local girl making good in the big city was headline news and I've been wanting to stop in and lend a little support, congratulate them on the venture. That sort of thing." He looked around for a familiar face but the place was manned this evening by two teenagers. "Guess neither of them are here tonight."

"Maybe you can leave them a note," Jennifer said as she scanned the offerings on the board behind the counter. She was surprised to see they included a selection of frozen yogurt and sherberts as well as a dozen or more specialty flavors beyond the standard chocolate, strawberry and vanilla. "That's quite a selection. They ought to do well."

Steve favored her with a slow grin, then drawled, "We country folks try to do our best when it comes to impressing you city slickers. We go all out if it's necessary."

"Is that what you're trying to do?" The question had tripped off her tongue as if it had a will of its own. Jennifer would have given just about anything to call it back. She'd provided the perfect opening back to the subject they'd gotten into before dinner. It was the last thing she'd wanted to do.

The heated look Steve gave her should have melted every tub of frozen confection behind the counter. "You better know it," he replied, drawling again. Delivered low, just loud enough for only her to hear, he said, "I'm after you, Jennifer Lewis, and I'm going to do whatever it takes to have you."

Jennifer gulped and concentrated on keeping her legs steady enough to hold her up. If moments before he'd been casting her as a city sophisticate and himself as an inexperienced country boy, he'd just rewritten the script and the new characterizations seemed truer to life.

If she were truly an experienced city sophisticate, she would have been able to deliver a clever comeback. But she wasn't at all experienced in repartee or anything else involved in a man-woman relationship. The pretty teenagers behind the counter, young women a little more than half her age, were probably better skilled in dealing with the opposite sex than she was.

Professionally Jennifer could think as quickly on her feet as any of her colleagues regardless of their sex. In the courtroom or at the negotiating table, nothing intimidated her. Standing in a small neighborhood ice-cream parlor, her mind totally blank, her palms sweaty, her pulse rate accelerated, she felt like a caricature of a country innocent who'd just been propositioned by a sophisticated wolf from the city.

Unwittingly one of the teenagers came to her rescue right then by asking if she was ready to order. "Er...ah...French Vanilla...one dip."

"Understated elegance, just like you," Steve quipped. "Ordinary old chocolate, a double dip, for this country boy."

There was nothing ordinary about him or the sinfully rich chocolate ice cream he was served. The way he watched her lap a drip of ice cream sliding down her cone, then without ever shifting his gaze from hers, repeated the same action himself was as arousing as any kiss or caress they'd shared in the past several weeks. Suddenly feeling so warm and liquidy she feared her legs wouldn't hold her, Jennifer quickly sought one of the wire chairs at the closest table.

Steve followed suit, adjusting Stephanie's sling carrier as he settled into the dainty chair opposite her. Jennifer wished her daughter would make some sort of fuss to provide diversion, but Stephanie, though bright-eyed and completely awake, was totally content against Steve's chest.

Though the intimacy they'd had in the past had just occurred naturally and unplanned, Jennifer's lack of experience didn't keep her from recognizing that she was being openly and steadily seduced with each passing moment.

He didn't touch her. He didn't have to. His eyes caressed her. His voice and tone, rather than the words he uttered, aroused her. At first Jennifer was exceedingly grateful that they were in a public place, but then an increasingly large part of her began wishing she had a magic wand and could transport them with a blink of an eye back to the privacy of her house. The vanilla-laced confection she was making her way through could have been sawdust for all she could taste.

"Ready?"

"No!" she blurted, then caught the look of puzzlement on Steve's face. Quickly cramming the last of her cone into her mouth, she chewed and said, "Now I am." She glanced at her watch. "Perfect timing. Stephanie ought to be ready for her evening snack by the time we get back."

"Then she's out for the night?" Steve inquired and Jennifer shivered in reaction to the hope she heard in his voice.

Nine

Aware of Jennifer hovering near the doorway, Steve lowered the newspaper he'd been pretending to read ever since they'd returned from the ice-cream parlor. "Stephanie asleep already?" he asked.

"All that fresh air must have tired her out. She went down with absolutely no fuss tonight. In fact I think I was keeping her awake."

"It's good for babies to get outside, breathe the fresh air, enjoy the sunshine," he said.

Jennifer dropped down to her knees on the floor beside the quilt she'd spread out earlier for Stephanie and began gathering the assortment of rattles and stuffed animals scattered there. She placed the toys in a basket and started folding the quilt. "There wasn't much sunshine this evening, but she certainly enjoyed the outing nonetheless," she commented though her mind was more attuned to every nuance of the man seated a few feet away.

His intentions for the rest of the evening couldn't have been more clear. Just as clear was the message her own body was sending her that she was scared to death.

What are you afraid of, Jennifer? Steve's question haunted her but it was her own conscience that was asking, as she spent an inordinate amount of time lining up the corners of the quilt and folding it ever so neatly and ever so slowly. Intimacy had been inevitable since their first kiss. If not then, certainly after the increasingly more frequent and lengthy ones that had been building more heatedly at the end of each evening they spent together.

Hadn't she been yearning for this more nights than she could name in recent weeks, even planned for it? Physically she was ready. Dr. Canfield had released her to resume all normal activities weeks ago. He'd even written out a prescription for birth control pills, warning her against getting pregnant again for several months even with the possible infertility looming over her head.

"Birth control . . . ?" Jennifer had almost laughed in the office but had refrained from it and from giving a reminder of how she'd gotten pregnant. She might have just given birth but it had been more than a dozen years since she'd been intimate with a man.

Until Steve there hadn't been anyone she'd given even a second's thought to sharing a bed. And if it hadn't been for Steve she would have tossed the prescription away. She'd wanted Stephanie with all her heart, even wished she could have a half dozen more and give Stephanie the kind of childhood she herself had wanted. But, given her body's condition and the hardship of combining a career with single parenting, she'd convinced herself to be content with only one child.

Until Steve she'd wondered if she was still capable of feeling desire for a man. Since law school when she'd given her body and a part of her heart to a fellow student who hadn't wanted either for very long, she'd buried her hurt deeply by immersing herself in her work. She didn't think she'd even had an erotic dream in the interim before Steve Barthelmaus had come into her life.

Steve was everything she'd once dreamed of finding in a man. And that was exactly what pulled her toward him one moment and made her perversely shy away from him the next. Keeping her distance would protect her from hurt, but she wouldn't have a chance at possible joy, either. What was the cliché? You can't win the contest unless you enter?

"Jennifer...?"

Steve's voice startled her out of her thoughts and Jennifer rose on shaky legs. "I...I'll be back in a moment." She clutched the quilt protectively to her chest and said, "This belongs in the baby's room."

Steve reached over, plucked the quilt from her arms and tossed it on a chair. "Leave it," he ordered gently as he tugged Jennifer down to the cushion beside him. "You'll just have to bring it back out again tomorrow."

Jennifer raised wide eyes and started to argue. "But, it's—"

"A tiny bit of clutter," Steve finished for her. "In fact it adds a homey touch."

"You think this room is cold?"

Steve glanced around the room, knowing exactly what he would see. The colors of the walls, carpeting and furniture were a tasteful blend of dusty shades of coral, jade and cream. Even the paintings and objets d'art matched. Everything was perfectly coordinated and everything was in its place—a reflection of the woman who lived there.

Except for that drab hospital gown, everything he'd ever seen Jennifer wear was attractive and well put together. Each garment and accessory was color and style coordinated. This evening was no exception. Her low-heeled shoes were the same shade of blue as her sweater. A blue enameled bracelet ringed one of her slender wrists. Small disk earrings of blue enameled metal with a brush stroke of white decorated her earlobes.

He loved the way she dressed and could appreciate the reasons why. Knowing she'd grown up in foster homes and then put herself through college and law school, he found it easy to surmise that she'd had a fraction of the clothes and shoes his sisters had "needed." He could also guess that much of what she'd had during her early years had been secondhand, which explained why now everything was new and meticulously maintained.

However, he would love to see her thoroughly disheveled once in a while. More than once in a while, he corrected. He wanted to see her hair tumbled from the stroke of his hands, her lips bruised from his kisses and her body wearing nothing but the flush of satisfaction he'd just given her. And what he really wanted was to see her like that every night, beginning tonight.

"The room is perfect," he said pushing his last thought temporarily out of his mind. He'd been charged with a quest this evening and he'd put it off long enough. He dropped his arm around her shoulders and pulled her against him. "But back to sunshine. You do think sunshine is good for babies, don't you?"

Jennifer wasn't sure whether to laugh, cry or scream in frustration. She'd spent the better part of the past hour preparing herself to be seduced and Steve was talking about the merits of sunshine on babies. What had happened to the man who'd made the eating of ice-cream cones an act of seduction? And men thought women had mood swings!

"Of course I think sunshine is good for babies. I've been taking Stephanie for walks and we've been spending a little time out in the sun almost every day."

"And fresh air?"

"Great."

"How about country fresh air?"

"I suppose it's very good for babies."

"Good. I knew I could convince you sooner or later," he announced and squeezed her shoulder.

"Convince me . . . ?" Jennifer scooted forward and turned so she was squarely facing him. "What is this all about?"

"The Fourth of July's coming up. Though Mom and Dad are out in Arizona, the rest of us still get together for a day-long celebration, beginning with the parade down Main Street in the morning. Then we gather at the farm, picnic all day, play a little softball, volleyball, whatever strikes us before we take in the fireworks. My sisters and I have always brought friends to the gathering. I'd like you and Stephanie to share it with us this year.''

Steve wasn't surprised to see Jennifer visibly shrink at the prospect of participating in what he'd just described. "I know it sounds pretty overwhelming, but it's really relaxed," he quickly assured.

Not meeting his eyes, she said, "It...uh...sounds lovely, but Lanine and her husband are having a party at their house for the holiday." She hadn't exactly told a lie. Lanine and her husband were hosting a neighborhood party on the Fourth. She'd mentioned it the day before when she'd delivered the stack of briefs and contracts Jennifer had requested. However, having weeks ago wheedled the information out of Jennifer that Steve was a steady visitor, she'd made it very clear that she assumed Jennifer would be spending the day with Steve.

Steve's family's plans did sound like the all-American celebration. But she just couldn't face it. What could she possibly talk about with his sisters and brothers-in-law all day? No matter how relaxed Steve might think the day would be, she knew she'd be a bundle of nerves. Overwhelming? You bet!

"Can't you tell Lanine you have other plans?"

He had such a look of hope in his eyes, Jennifer felt herself weakening. "I don't know, Steve," she hedged.

"Say you'll spend the day with me, please," he coaxed. "It'll be good for you and the baby. Fresh country air, sunshine and lots of food and even more fun.

"You won't even have to pack much stuff for the baby," he threw in for what he hoped was enticement. "Mom set up one of the bedrooms as a nursery for the grandkids years ago and since I didn't need that room for anything, it's pretty much the way it was when Karen's and Lisa's kids were babies. There's even a playpen and a swing we can put her in when we're all outside.''

Contemplating going to bed with Steve had been one thing. Meeting his family all at once and spending an entire day with them was quite another, especially at the place he so casually referred to as the farm. It was a different kind of intimacy, somehow deeper and thus all the more frightening.

He'd told her so much about the farm and the plans he had for it. It was the Barthelmaus ancestral home. The land had supported three generations and the house had sheltered them. It now awaited the fourth— Steve's children. The thought of putting Stephanie in a crib the Barthelmaus's grandchildren had used caused a lump to form in her throat. It was all too perfect, too close to the kind of roots and traditions she'd always dreamed of.

Desperate to put several feet between herself and Steve's disturbing presence, Jennifer started to rise but Steve's strong hands snaked around her waist and held her in place. "No trumped-up excuses this time," he said and Jennifer wondered if he'd sensed the truth about Lanine's party. "I won't take no for an answer. I can't afford to and neither can you unless you want the clan to descend upon you here."

Jennifer shook her head slowly. "They wouldn't."

"They would. Lisa and Karen are determined to meet the woman who's been enticing me into the city almost every evening for the past two months."

"I haven't been enticing you anywhere," Jennifer demurred, thinking of all the ways she'd tried to convince Steve to stay away.

A seductive smile played at the corners of his mouth and his eyes took on the darkened eroticism he'd bestowed on her at the ice-cream parlor. "Lady, no siren ever enticed a sailor more effectively. You're not even realizing your powers over a man make you all the more alluring."

"Me? Powers over a man?"

Jennifer wasn't fishing for more compliments and Steve knew it from more than her wide-eyed guileless expression. She honestly didn't realize how very sexy she was. Other men were surely aware of it. What was hard for him to believe was that he hadn't had to fend off dozens of men to get to her and that she'd had to resort to artificial insemination to have a baby.

"Believe it, Jennifer," he said and tugged her toward him, groaning his pleasure when she fell forward and her soft breasts flattened against his chest. "And believe you're going to enjoy this holiday—at the farm."

Any protest she might have presented he stifled by taking immediate possession of her delectable mouth.

The tip of his tongue against her lips stoked the embers he'd lit earlier, bringing them quickly to flame. She hesitated only a second or two before opening to him. His tongue probed her mouth until she was on fire and felt compelled to return his devouring exploration. His taste was more delicious than any flavor of ice cream anyone had ever invented and she hungered for more.

Unable to resist the enticing hard contours of his chest beneath her palms, she explored them thoroughly before moving to his shoulders. Finally she played her fingers along the strong column of his neck and through the silky hairs at his nape.

Arching her body against him and seeking a greater closeness was as natural as breathing and she knew he was mistaken in calling her a siren. He had given the siren call she was unable to resist. His voice, his taste and the touch of his hands on her body were rendering her mindless with a need that had been building for weeks.

Steve adjusted their positions until they lay beside each other on the couch. His strong hands pulled her softness to him then sent flashes of pleasure through her when they molded her waist and buttocks. His thumbs traced the line of her hips then moved to the hem of her sweater.

"I want to make love to you, Jennifer," he said huskily. "Completely. Are you ready for that?"

Though a tiny part of her still feared she was risking heartbreak again, Jennifer nodded.

Steve took a deep breath then asked, "Are you sure?"

"I'm sure that I want you to make love to me," she said and knew that it was the complete truth. Having already wrestled the demons of uncertainty, she was prepared for this moment. Whatever the future might bring, she'd have this memory and if she protected her heart very carefully, she'd not be destroyed by disappointment when their relationship ended.

Without another word Steve rolled off the couch then bent over to lift her. Jennifer wrapped trembling arms around his shoulders and pressed her face into the crook of his neck as he carried her into her bedroom. Beside her bed, he set her on her feet again.

Steadying herself, she placed her hands on each side of his waist. "I've dreamed of you, Steve," she admitted aloud, but kept it her own secret that the dream had been forming all her life.

His eyes glittered with a trace of humor as he smiled. "You weren't the only one dreaming, sweetheart. I've been having dreams for weeks. And sleepless nights when thoughts of you kept me awake."

"I'm sorry."

He chuckled low and deep. "I'm not. They were great dreams and now every one of them and all the late-night thoughts are about to come true."

Worry that she'd disappoint him made her shudder. "Steve, I...I may disappoint you. It's been a long time for me and I...I was never very good at sex."

His smile was so sweet, Jennifer felt tears threaten behind her eyes. "You won't disappoint me, Jennifer. We're going to make love not sex and I think you're going to be very good at it." He raised his hands and cradled her face between his palms before bending to place a soft kiss on her lips. "I'm going to try to go very, very slowly and do my best to make this a night we'll both remember for the rest of our lives."

He moved his hands to the hem of her sweater and slowly and carefully eased it up and away from her body. In the dim light shining from a small lamp in the hallway, he could see the gentle rise of her breasts above the delicate lace of her bra. He ran his fingertips across the soft skin, then bent and slid his warm mouth along the same path. A brush of his thumb released the fastening between her breasts and spilled their fullness to his waiting palms. Wriggling her shoulders, Jennifer rid herself of the wisp of lace and elastic and it slid to the floor.

"You are a dream," Steve murmured against one throbbing nipple before he took it into his mouth.

Jennifer's senses reeled and she nearly fainted. His tongue was so arousing. It felt so good, she quivered and would have sunk to the floor if Steve hadn't caught her waist with his hands. "Your turn," he said.

Her fingers fumbled with the two buttons at the top of his knit shirt, then she slid her hands down his chest until she encountered the waistband of his pants. Tugging, she managed to free his shirt. With a little help from Steve, she skimmed it over his head and tossed it toward a chair in a corner.

And then she hesitated, unsure of how to proceed. Prior experience had been hurried and always in complete darkness. There had been very little foreplay and never this slow, leisurely disrobing.

Steve's torso was beautiful. His skin was smooth, hazed only lightly with a patch of golden hair on his chest. His shoulders were wide, and she knew without touching him that his abdomen was hard with muscle. A narrow shadow of dark gold hair began there and disappeared beneath the waistband of his pants. He was so male she shivered.

Steve caught her hands, pressed them to his chest and urged her with, "I want you to touch me as I've touched you. I want to feel your hands and your mouth on me."

Granting his wishes, Jennifer let her fingers glide across the contours she'd just admired. Emboldened by his words and the lesson he'd just taught her, she let her lips discover the wonders of his chest and flick her tongue across the hardened nubs of his flat nipples.

"Ah . . . Jennifer, you could never be a disappointment," Steve said just before taking her mouth again. He wooed her lips as he'd done before, softly enticing them open. His tongue swept inside while his hands slid down over her buttocks, lifted her up and fit her against him.

The feel of his flesh against hers made her want to cry out. She could sense the hot and hard evidence of his arousal through the remaining fabric between them and understood the power he'd told her she wielded over him. She reveled in knowing that she was, indeed, womanly and very desirable.

But this was only a beginning. Taking turns they divested each other of their clothing until they stood naked and vulnerable before each other. The sight of him, so strong, uncompromisingly male and blatantly aroused filled her with an unbearable tension that turned to melting sweetness when he laid her gently upon the bed and kissed and stroked his way from her ankles to her throat.

Pausing briefly to ask if she was protected, he covered her with his body and sought her mouth again. As his fingers feathered lightly over the hidden mount of her desire, his tongue enticed hers to twine and tease his. Soon, his fingers had teased and stroked her to an overpowering urgency and she wrapped her arms around him, wanting to blend her body with his.

Restless with the increasing yearning he was building within her, Jennifer splayed her hands across his buttocks, pressing him closer, impatient for fulfillment. Steve's lips tasted her sweet moans of longing. He blended them with his own as he pushed carefully into her softness and claimed her.

Bridling the primitive needs raging within him, he rocked gently against her. Jennifer sighed his name and matched his motion, arching to meet him more eagerly with each thrust. Soon, the rhythm intensified and Jennifer cried out with such abandon, Steve could no longer control his passion.

Together they built the momentum that catapulted them to a joyous release. Shaking in the aftermath, they clung together. Limbs intertwined, hearts pounding in unison, their bodies covered with a moist sheen, they floated downward from the summit until at last their labored breathing returned to normal.

Bracing himself on his elbows, Steve took his weight off Jennifer's body. "Are you okay?" he asked, worried that when he'd lost control, he'd hurt her.

The large gray eyes that gazed up at him reflected no pain and Steve felt his worry recede.

"I'm more than okay," Jennifer told him breathlessly. Smiling up at the man who'd given her such joy, she gathered up enough strength to press a light kiss on his chin. She dropped back to the pillow, so satiated her bones felt as if they'd turned to jelly. "That was—"

"Making love," Steve finished, thrilling her with his words and the way he was looking at her. "And you were very, very good at it."

He kissed her gently, then taking her with him, rolled over, settling her atop him. Tucking her head beneath his chin, he sifted his fingers through her hair. "I love your hair. It's fascinated me since the very first time I touched it."

Lifting a handful of the gold-streaked mass to his face he breathed deeply. "So silky and it smells so good. All of you smells good. Whatever that perfume is that you wear, somebody ought to tell the War Department about it."

Drowsily Jennifer mumbled, "Why would the War Department want to know about a line of iris-scented toiletries?"

Catching her chin with his fingers, Steve lifted her head until she could see his wicked grin. "It has the power to render strong men weak."

Testing her newly discovered power, Jennifer swiveled her breasts and then her hips against him. Steve groaned as he felt himself growing ready again. "Jennifer...?" he asked in a choking whisper.

Jennifer felt a thrill of female satisfaction as she felt the instant contraction of muscle in his flat belly and the hardness surging against her softness. "Have I really rendered you weak?" she teased, surprising herself that she could banter at a time like this. Until Steve had come into her life, she'd never initiated teasing under any circumstances, and it certainly hadn't been a part of the hurried sex of her one and only affair.

"Maybe not weak." He chuckled lightly and swept her beneath him again. A moment's concern for her prompted him to hold himself in check long enough to ask, "Are you really sure this is wise again, tonight? I don't want to hurt you."

Wise? Maybe not, but for different reasons than he was asking. "You won't hurt me, Steve," she said, though she feared he eventually would. Not physically, but in her heart. This wouldn't last. Nothing truly good had ever lasted in her life, and next to Stephanie, Steve was the best thing that had ever happened to her.

Putting aside her fears for the future, she wound her arms around his shoulders and smiled up at him. "You promised this would be a night to remember, didn't you?'' she asked, hoping the memory of this night would balance against the abandonment and loneliness she'd inevitably suffer soon.

"We'll remember, sweetheart," he assured her. "We'll have every night to remind us and make even more memorable."

Every night was a wonderful thought, and Jennifer believed he meant it at the moment he said it. And so did she, when she echoed the sentiment. How ever many nights they'd have together would be memorable.

"Irises, huh?" he murmured against her breasts as he started them on another sensuous journey more wonderful than the first.

By the time they'd reached the lofty peaks again, Jennifer was in no doubt that Steve's lovemaking would be something she'd remember for the rest of her life. If she was very lucky, sometime long after he was gone, and the pain of loss had ebbed, she'd be able to treat the memories the same way she'd treated her book of fairy tales. A pretty story, set in a faraway land of dreams. Like Cinderella at the ball she'd have this time with the handsome prince, but when midnight arrived, that would be the end of her story.

Ten

Glancing once more at the map Steve had drawn for her, Jennifer assured herself she was still on course. "One more turn, and I think we'll be there, Stephie."

Driving herself and Stephanie up to the farm this morning had seemed the logical thing to do when she'd suggested it. It would have been silly for Steve to drive into Columbus, pick them up, then drive right straight back to Delaware. That had been the logic she'd presented to Steve when they, or rather he, had firmed up plans for Independence Day. In truth she'd wanted her own car with her as a token of independence. She felt a little more in control knowing she had her own transportation and could make a quick getaway whenever she felt it necessary.

As the day had loomed closer and closer, she'd tried to wiggle out of the invitation, but hadn't been able to come up with a good enough excuse.

"I never did really accept, you know," she grumbled to herself as she drove along the country road. "You just assumed my answer was yes because you think it's the right thing to do."

Venting her ire verbally was making her feel a little less impotent, even if the person she was directing it toward wasn't there. "Pushy, that's what you are. You just take over and think you know better than I do what's best for Stephie and me, and spineless me has been letting you. All you have to do is give me one of your melty-eyed looks or kiss me and I jump right through whatever hoop you're holding."

That was an exaggeration, but she was on a roll and it felt good.

"Spending from dawn till dusk with your family is not what's best for us, Dr. Barthelmaus! Maybe we're allergic to country air. All that hay and grass and who knows what else. Did you ever consider that? No? I'll just bet you didn't.

"Lord, now you've got me talking to myself and answering, too." She smacked the steering wheel with the palm of her hand. "Steven Barthelmaus you've driven me over the edge."

Narrowing her eyes on the horizon, she glared at the paleness of the morning sun. "Whoever decided Fourth of July parades should start early in the morning ought to be hung," she complained.

Allowing for the holiday traffic congestion in Columbus, travel time to Steve's farm, transferring to his car and driving into the town of Delaware, she'd had to leave her house just after seven. Yawning, she reached for the mug of coffee secured in a niche in the console beside her.

"I'm not used to being dressed and out of the house this early in the morning, Steph. Your mother's gotten used to puttsing around in her nightgown and robe in the morning." Looking over at the baby snoozing in the carrier strapped into the passenger seat, she said, "Lucky you. You're getting your morning nap, anyway. Sleep while you can, sweetheart. It's going to be quite a day."

Turning onto the last road change before Steve's driveway, Jennifer checked her odometer. "One more mile from this point and then a sign I'm not supposed to be able to miss."

Her stomach began to tighten and her palms grew slippery on the steering wheel. Insecurity about her ability to spend a whole day with strangers grew stronger with each fence post she passed. She'd never been good at small talk, so what was she going to do all day? Had she packed enough diapers, formula and clothing for Stephanie? Had she dressed them both properly?

Though the weather report had predicted a perfect Fourth of July, sunny and in the high eighties, the temperature had been cool when she'd left the house. She'd grabbed a cotton cardigan for herself and thrown it over her red sleeveless tank top and white walking shorts. She'd slipped a tiny sweater over Stephanie's red, white and blue romper suit and tossed a light blanket over her legs. Had she remembered the baby's hat, her own sunglasses? It would be bright once the sun really came up.

Stephanie was normally a very good baby, but what if she chose to be fussy today? New surroundings, new people. Stephanie wasn't any more used to them than her mother was. Maybe the baby would start screaming her head off, and then she'd have the perfect excuse to pack up and head back to Columbus. Or maybe her mother would do the screaming.

"Oh Lord, there it is," Jennifer said under her breath when she saw a large white sign on the right side of the road.

> Steven C. Barthelmaus, D.V.M.
> Veterinary Clinic
> Animal Hospital
> Boarding Kennels and Stables

Overriding a cowardly need to turn around and head back to Columbus, Jennifer turned into the driveway. Perched on a hill, the two-story house was white-painted brick with black shutters. An open porch stretched along one side. The overall design was fairly typical of farmhouses of its era and locale, and yet it had a little bit more formality and graciousness about it than most. Large spirea bushes bordered two sides of the house, and several huge spreading trees shaded the yard. Again, typical plantings, but the added touch of brick walkways bordered with an assortment of flowers provided a riot of color that set the house apart from its more simple sisters.

Following the directive at a fork in the road, she veered to the left toward the house and drew to a stop beside the walkway leading to the side door. She could see Steve's clinic, the stable and what appeared to be miles of high white fences stretching out beyond. It was quite an impressive spread. The buildings were well kept and the grounds tidy and well-groomed. The farm, as Steve called it, fell just enough short of being a showplace to not be intimidating and so close to her childhood dreams she felt as if she'd just driven into either the *Twilight Zone* or paradise.

A tapping on the car window beside her startled her out of her reverie. Steve's smile was from ear to ear as he opened her door. "Happy Fourth!" he greeted enthusiastically as he helped her out. Enfolding her as soon as her feet were on the ground, he kissed her quickly and continued to hold her close. "God, I'm glad you two are finally here."

"Are we late?"

"No, you're even ahead of time." He leaned his head against the top of her head. "I was just a little worried that's all. Thought you might get lost or stuck in the holiday traffic and I was afraid—" He stopped whatever he'd been about to say and finished with "You're here. That's the main thing."

Jennifer moved out of his arms so she could look at him. There was a slight tightening around his eyes, and an anxious look about his features in general. "What were you afraid of? That we might not come?"

"Well...er...ah...yeah."

"Good!" She glared at him but almost hooted with glee. "There's hope for you yet. Maybe you do have a conscience after all."

Looking like the epitome of innocence, Steve asked, "What would I have to feel guilty about?"

Jennifer pierced him with a narrow-eyed glare. "Overall pushy nature in general and not really giving me a choice about today specifically." Stepping past him, she moved to the other side of the car and started unstrapping the baby. "Do we have time for a cup of coffee before we take in the parade?"

Steve was right behind her, unloading the diaper bag and other gear she'd tossed in the back seat. "Plenty of time. I can only provide instant but I can accompany it with a slice of Marian's coffee cake. Guaranteed to put a smile on the sourest face." He started up the walkway toward the house.

"Are you insulting me?"

"I didn't mean to." He opened one of the atrium doors leading off the porch and stepped aside for Jennifer and the baby to pass. "What's gotten into you this morning? The last time I saw you, you were the sweetest, warmest bundle of womanhood a man could ever pray for. This morning you're about as cuddly as a grizzly bear who just crawled out of a cave."

Feeling her cheeks heat up, Jennifer ducked her head as she stepped through the doorway and into an utterly charming room. Wicker furniture, chairs, a sofa and a chaise lounge, upholstered with a bold navy and white plaid, provided comfortable seating. Ferns and other trailing plants, some with bright blossoms, hung from the skylighted ceiling. A thick Berber rug decorated the center of the quarry tile floor.

The room was so enchanting that for a moment she forgot her embarrassment—but only for a moment.... "You've never seen me in the early morning," she offered, hoping he wouldn't delve further. "I'm not much of a morning person now that I have Stephanie." She really didn't want to discuss the contrast between her attitude toward Steve this morning and the last time he'd seen her.

It had been three nights ago and Steve had stayed until the wee hours of the morning. Remembrances of how she'd responded with abandon to his lovemaking washed over her and the blush she knew was coloring her cheeks spread through her body. If Stephanie hadn't awakened for her 3:00 a.m. feeding, Steve might have been in her bed for several more hours and it wouldn't have been for sleeping.

That he'd had emergencies the following evenings, preventing him from coming to her house had been fortunate. At first she'd been disappointed when he'd called to explain where he was but then the disappointment had turned to relief. She'd needed the time to recover her good sense and put her affair with Steve into proper perspective. An affair. That's all it was. And if she could gather the courage, she was going to end it this very day. Coming at all and putting herself through the torture of meeting his family was a big mistake.

Spreading out an extra receiving blanket on the sofa, Jennifer busied herself changing the baby's diaper and giving herself a chance to think what she should do. She was here and she really didn't feel like turning around and fighting the traffic to get back into the city. She didn't want to spoil the celebrations for Steve. He'd described everything with such enthusiasm; he had obviously really been looking forward to this holiday. She might as well muddle through the day and then find a way to break things off.

Out of the corner of her eye she saw Steve carrying a tray holding two mugs of coffee and a plate heaped with thick wedges of cinnamon-marbled coffee cake, which he placed on the big flat-topped trunk that served as a cocktail table.

As soon as she'd settled the baby into the infant seat and satisfied herself the device was in no danger of slipping off the trunk, Steve handed her one of the steaming mugs. "Drink up." After picking up the other mug, he settled himself on the opposite end of the sofa. He waited until she'd taken a sip of coffee. "So what's really bothering you?"

"I told you. It's too early in the morning for me to be pleasant."

Steve's expression revealed his skepticism, but he let it pass without comment. "Well, get a little more caffeine in you, have a piece of cake and then we'll pack up for the parade. It's sure to put you in the holiday mood. Our town throws a great parade. Most of the county participates in some way. And the fireworks tonight may not be as spectacular as Columbus's Red, White and Boom display, but they're still a pretty good show."

Steve was trying so hard to spark some enthusiasm in her, Jennifer forced a smile. "Okay, okay, you've convinced me I'm going to have a great time. Go on out and transfer Stephanie's car seat to your car and let me finish my coffee in a little peace. We'll be out by the time you're done."

Steve grinned at her. "That's my girl." Standing up, he leaned over her and gave her a swift peck on the lips. "You won't be sorry you came today, sweetheart. I promise."

With a stab of guilt Jennifer watched him bound out the door and across the porch. He'd called her sweetheart again and she knew that's how he thought of her. She was going through with the festivities on false pretenses.

This day was going to mark independence, all right—hers from Steve. But she didn't feel much like celebrating.

Lying on a blanket under one of the big shade trees, Jennifer listened to Steve play with the baby. She kept her eyes closed, pretending to be getting the rest she'd claimed she needed. It was only a little after three in the afternoon, but it felt as if they'd already put in a full day.

They'd joined Steve's sisters and their families in town to watch the parade. Brunch back at the farm had followed, which had been attended by not only his family, but most of his staff and their families plus an assortment of neighbors and friends. In all, there had to have been fifty people gathered around the long tables of food that had been set up in minutes after their return from town.

The small talk Jennifer had dreaded hadn't been difficult at all. Everyone had been so friendly, and with such a big crowd she hadn't been required to talk with any one person for very long. Karen had plucked Stephanie immediately out of Jennifer's arms and so rhapsodized over her, all Jennifer had had to do was stand by and accept the compliments. Then it had been Lisa's turn and after that Stephanie had passed from one new set of arms to another. Accepting her role as the star of the day, Stephanie had smiled and cooed to the delight of each new fan doing his or her best to amuse her.

Steve's nieces and nephews were just as delightful as their mothers. They were healthy, outgoing children, polite, but full of enough impish exuberance to be real. Jennifer knew she was in danger of losing her heart to each and every member of Steve's family. Even Steve's brothers-in-law were charming with their good-natured teasing back and forth and their gentle ways with the children.

The wild game of softball that had followed brunch was something she'd never forget. Nobody was left out. Because of the crowd, sometimes two or more people played a position. Considering that some of the players were as young as four years old, errors were more common than good plays. Fun was the only object of the game, and Jennifer had had fun. She'd managed a respectable hit at her time up to bat and caught a fly ball hit by Steve to the cheering delight of his sisters.

She was having a great time. But Steve was wrong when he said she wouldn't be sorry she came. She was growing more and more sorry with each passing hour. This little tableau under the tree was adding to her misery.

The tree sheltering them from the late-afternoon sun didn't have pink blossoms, and there was a babble of happy voices not far away, rather than the call of a bird. Those were small, insignificant details. The scene was still so close to the one she'd dreamed the day Stephanie was born, she wanted to cry. And so she kept her eyelids sealed tightly, as much to shut out the reality around her as to hang on to the dream for just a little while longer.

Something warm and moist brushing against her lips brought her eyes open. Steve was leaning over her, his face filling her range of vision. "Hi," he said softly. "Have a good nap?"

Blinking her eyes, Jennifer was startled out of the fog she hadn't meant to fall into. "Where's Stephanie?"

He smiled and brushed her lips with his again. "With Lisa. She came over a while ago and took her away from me."

Jennifer tried to get up but Steve pushed her shoulders back down on the blanket, then trapped her there with the light pressure of his own chest. "Steve, please." She pushed against him but couldn't budge him. "Stephanie must be sopping wet and hungry by now. I've got to get to her."

"Relax. She's in good hands. Lisa and Karen have already seen to all of that."

She tried to protest but Steve placed a silencing finger over her lips. "My sisters adore babies. They're having a wonderful time. Don't go snatch her away from them. Besides, you've got better things to do with your time."

"Like what?"

"This for starters."

With only that little warning, Steve lowered his head to her startled lips. He took possession of her mouth quickly, invading its soft interior with the full thrust of his tongue after only a minimum of coaxing her to open to him. Stroking the delicate surfaces he'd conquered, he delved deeper and deeper inside with a rhythm that was a microcosmic act of love.

Jennifer's head was swimming and her breath was coming in irregular gasps when he lifted his head. "Steve!" She shoved his shoulders, this time managing to put a little space between them. "It's broad daylight and there are dozens of people around."

"No there aren't," he murmured against her temple and began raining tiny kisses on her that led down toward her throat. "Some people have left and those who are still here are gathered around the practice track watching Don put Blaze through her paces. Nobody'll be back up for at least another half hour."

Jennifer shivered as Steve nibbled the edges of her tank top and ran the tip of his tongue along the upper rise of her breasts. She could feel her nipples tighten with anticipation, and her body began to quiver with a need she knew he could appease so well. While she could still think straight, she slithered out from under him and sat up.

Steve reached for her but Jennifer scooted farther away. "Don't. This is not the time or the place."

With a sigh of obvious regret, Steve rolled to his side and propped his head in his hand. His grin was cocky. "I can think of a lot better place and better time. Let's forget the fireworks and make our own."

In reaction to his sensuous suggestion, Jennifer pulled her knees up and wrapped her arms around them. Her body coiled into a near fetal position, she felt more protected from the invitations his eyes, lips and voice were giving her. Not for anything was she going to comment on his suggestion. Looking around her, she noticed how long the shadows were. "Shouldn't you be starting the charcoal for the hot dogs?"

Steve groaned and flopped onto his back. "How can you mention more food?"

Jennifer shrugged. The thought of another meal wasn't very appealing to her stomach after the orgy that had started out as brunch, moved directly into lunch and ended with "snacks" between innings. But the activity would provide a welcome diversion. "Rick mentioned that it was a tradition and you're the appointed chef. You don't want to disappoint anyone do you?"

"Heaven forbid." He heaved himself to his feet then stretched a helping hand out to her. "Come on, you can help me get the fire started. The quicker we get it going, the quicker we'll get supper over with and then we can be rid of all these people."

Including me! There was no way she was going to stay after everyone else had left. As enticing as Steve's description of his plans for later on were, she wasn't going to be here for them. She wasn't going to risk another night in his arms.

Jennifer let him help her up but shrugged away from the arm he tried to slip around her waist. God knew she needed the support, for her knees were still shaky in the aftermath of that kiss. However, having his arm around her and pulling her up against his side would only make her senses more crazed than they already were.

"You're on your own with the fire," she said as she headed for the stables. "It's time I let my daughter know her mother hasn't deserted her."

"Later, sweetheart," he called after her. "Escape while you can, but we're going to get some things settled before the fireworks."

Eleven

Cradled in her mother's lap, Stephanie was taking an inordinate amount of time getting her bottle down, to Jennifer's way of thinking. *Stephanie, your timing is lousy. Have you no sense of family loyalty?* While trying to remain placid so as not to upset her child, Jennifer willed the baby to sense her thoughts.

It was dusk. The house and grounds were nearly empty of people. Only Karen and her family remained...and Steve. The chance for unnoticed escape was long past. But Jennifer still harbored a small hope that Rick Kegan would keep Steve distracted long enough out on the patio for her to make an unheralded exit.

"Come on, Stephie, quit playing around," Jennifer coaxed when the baby pushed the nipple out of her mouth and turned her head to look around the room. She'd taken only a couple of ounces and Jennifer knew she was nowhere near finished. She pushed the nipple back into the baby's mouth and was momentarily gratified when Stephanie latched on to it with some eagerness. Unfortunately her eagerness lasted through only another half ounce, then she was back to looking around.

"She's had a lot of excitement today," Karen called from the kitchen where she was washing up the assortment of nondisposable items that had been used throughout the day.

"I don't think she's ever going to settle down tonight." Jennifer couldn't keep the dismay from her voice.

"She'll probably go out like a light as soon as we're all gone. I'll be done here in a couple of minutes, then I'll gather up the family and we'll be off. Shouldn't be but another five minutes and you'll have plenty of peace and quiet, I promise. Steve mentioned that you two are probably going to skip the fireworks and I think that's a good idea. Your baby's been a gem all day. Dragging her out this evening's pushing your luck."

Luck? Jennifer hadn't had any for the past couple of hours. Every time she'd thought she could sneak off, she'd been trapped. Someone had engaged her in conversation in such a way that only extreme rudeness on her part would have brought an end to it, or Steve had slipped up behind her, wrapped an arm around her waist and kept her beside him until his duties as host called him away.

Finally her own flesh and blood had plotted against her. When Jennifer had managed to locate her daughter and head for the house on the pretext of changing her, Stephanie had started gnawing on her hands as if she were ravenous. She shouldn't have needed another feeding for at least an hour—more than enough time for Jennifer to get them both back home.

We're going to get some things settled before the fireworks. Steve's words were haunting her. Her imagination had been working overtime trying to define what he thought needed to be settled between them. The only thing she could come up with was a discussion of where these alleged fireworks of theirs were going to take place—his house or hers.

"Done!" Karen announced, dropping down in the chair beside Jennifer's. Reaching over, she cupped her hand lightly over Stephanie's head. "She really is a darling, Jennifer. We're all so glad we finally got a chance to meet her—and you, too. Especially you!"

"It was nice to meet all of you, too," Jennifer said, wishing it wasn't so very true. "Steve's told me so much about the family. And I'd like to thank you in person for all the food you sent right after Stephanie and I came home from the hospital. That was very kind of you, and so much to do for someone you didn't even know."

Karen patted Jennifer's arm. "Well, we know you now and in case you haven't noticed, we've adopted you and the baby. We're looking forward to a lot more days like today."

The lump in Jennifer's throat prevented her from making a comment. She could only look up at Karen and offer what she knew was a wavery smile.

Karen gave her arm a little squeeze then jumped to her feet. "Hey, I promised we'd be out of here in five minutes, and I think I hear my family on their way in here to get me. I'll head 'em off, so they don't come trooping in here and get Stephanie all revved up again. Happy Fourth and we'll be seeing you soon."

"Happy Fourth," Jennifer returned but couldn't bring herself to lie and confirm that they'd be seeing each other soon.

Karen was at the door when she paused and turned back. "In case my brother didn't think of it, I made sure there were fresh linens on the crib upstairs. Since you've got Stephanie all ready for the night, as soon as she finishes that bottle, you can take her up. It's the second door on the right—you can't miss it."

"You're going to miss something if you don't get going." Steve pulled his sister none too gently through the door. "Your family's waiting in the car for you. Get out of here," he growled.

Karen's voice sounded from the edge of the porch. "You're very welcome, Stevie."

Chagrined, Steve called after her, "Hey thanks for all the food and staying to clean up the kitchen, Kae. Enjoy the fireworks."

Closing the door, he sauntered into the room and flopped down on the sofa opposite Jennifer. A ball of gray fur was tucked in the crook of his arm and the large shaggy dog that had followed him in had taken up a position at his feet. "Meet the rest of my family."

Dropping his hand to the dog's broad brown head, he scratched behind the animal's ears. "This is Sam. He's big but he's harmless." He resettled the ball of fur on his lap and gently stroked the animal Jennifer could now identify as a cat. "And this is Hugger. I told you about her, didn't I? Rescued her out from under the porch one cold winter night. Had a devil of a time convincing her I knew what was best for her."

"I sympathize with the cat," Jennifer mumbled.

Steve ignored the comment. "Both these beasties are a little shy, so I took them down to the kennels this morning before you arrived. Figured they'd be happier there than having to contend with a crowd of strangers."

"That was considerate of you." Jennifer didn't try to keep the sarcasm out of her voice.

"Today a little much?"

It had been, but not because of the size of the crowd. Shifting the baby to her shoulder, she patted Stephanie's back, hoping she didn't wake, for she'd finally fallen asleep. "We're both pretty tired," she announced starting up out of the chair. "I think it's time we headed back to Columbus."

"Oh no you don't." Steve tossed the cat aside and was beside Jennifer in a flash. Before she could stop him, he'd lifted Stephanie away from her and started through the kitchen with her. "Come on, this baby needs to be in bed, not riding in a car seat all the way back to Columbus."

"She'll sleep better in her own bed," Jennifer protested in a loud whisper, using every ounce of will to keep from shouting at him.

Steve kept right on going. "You heard Karen. That crib upstairs is magical. Babies love it."

Fuming, Jennifer followed at his heels. She'd known something like this would happen. "Don't you ever listen?"

"Sure. You said you were both tired. It makes absolutely no sense to drive all the way into the city tonight." He was already at the top of the stairs and turning down the hallway. "Catch the light beside you, will you?"

Jennifer followed this order unhesitatingly, but only because she didn't want to stumble around in the dark. "Come back here with my baby."

He didn't break stride, but disappeared through a doorway. She caught up with him just as he was spreading a blanket over the baby. "Are you really going to disturb her?" he asked, slipping his arm around Jennifer's waist the second she arrived at his side. "Look how contented she is."

Jennifer looked down at her sleeping daughter and knew defeat. Stephanie was sprawled out on her tummy looking every bit as content in the Barthelmaus family crib as she did in her own. It would be cruel to put her through the transfer to car, out of the car and into another house. The poor little baby had been handled so much this day, and with all the excitement she'd hardly slept. It was no wonder she was exhausted.

"My mom might have put the magic in this little bed," he whispered, his mouth so close his breath blew against the sensitive spot just behind her ear. She squirmed as a shiver of awareness snaked down her spine. Steve chuckled knowingly. "I'm taking the credit for the magic you're going to find in the bed you're spending the night in."

"You are the most egotistical, pushy, domineering, bossy—"

Steve moved away from the crib, tugging her along with him. "Let's talk about that somewhere else so we don't wake the baby."

Jennifer glared up at him. "You bet we're going to talk about it."

"That's my plan."

"Mine, too."

"Good." He opened another door in the hallway and pulled her inside. "Glad you realize tonight's the night," he said as he swept her up against him and sought her lips.

Jennifer angled her head and shoved his chest. "Not for that it's not," she told him sharply.

"Not right now, anyway," he said, dropping his arms from around her.

"Egotist!"

Steve chuckled as he crossed the darkened room and flipped on a lamp. Patting the quilt-covered mattress of a wide Paul Bunyan style bed, he invited, "Come on over here and we'll talk about what's happened between us."

"Not in here we're not," Jennifer declared as she turned on her heel. She'd had only a brief look at the room but it had been enough to warn her that it was Steve's bedroom.

"Coward," he said softly.

Jennifer's retreat came to an abrupt halt. Whirling, she placed her hands on her hips and stood her ground. "Look, you, wanting to have a serious conversation somewhere other than your bedroom isn't being cowardly. It's being sensible. Now are you coming downstairs or not?"

"It's a waste of time and energy to go back downstairs when we're going to end up here anyway."

"You're really sure of yourself, aren't you?" she said, her body trembling with fury.

"I'm sure that I love you."

Nothing he could have said would have surprised her more or so quickly put out the fire of her rage. Swallowing hard, she sought the support of the doorjamb. Shaking her head slowly as if she were in a daze,

she tamped down the joy that had leaped in her breast.
"No, you don't, Steve. You feel some sort of responsibility…a…uh…emotional high because of the baby,
but it's not love. You can't love me."

Steve had watched her closely during her little
speech and what he saw made him hurt. The pain and
fear he saw in her large expressive eyes cut right
through him. It was almost as if he were seeing the little foster child she'd been.

She'd said she'd grown up in foster homes. Not a
foster home, but homes. How many? Had there been
no one who had cared enough about her to keep her
for very long? "I can love you, Jennifer Lewis, and I
do. I plan on continuing to love you for the rest of my
life."

Jennifer continued to shake her head. She couldn't
let herself believe. "No."

"Yes," he said firmly and started moving slowly
toward her. "I want to marry you, Jennifer. I want
Stephanie to be my little girl, too. I want you and me
to give her a bunch of sisters and brothers so that this
house is filled up."

"But I may not be able to have more children,"
Jennifer said, thinking it only fair to remind him of
her possible infertility. "Stephanie may be the only
child I'll ever have."

"So? I couldn't love her any more than I already do,
and if you can't have more children and we decide we
want more, we can adopt."

Still shaking her head, Jennifer shrank into the
woodwork as he moved nearer. "You're an only son,"
she reminded him, needing to point out every possible reason he would be disappointed in her in
the future. "This farm has been in your family for

generations. You'll want to pass it on to your children."

"I want to pass it on to *our* children." Coming to a stop just inches from her, he cradled her face between his palms, forcing her to meet her eyes. "Our children," he repeated. "How we get them doesn't matter. What does matter is that we raise them together and with love. That's what will make them ours."

"Steve." She sighed, wanting so desperately to believe everything he was telling her.

"Do you love me, Jennifer?" He bent his head and kissed her lightly.

"I can't be a full-time mother, wife and homemaker like your sisters," she said, giving him what she thought was another reason to desert her.

"I'm not asking my sisters to marry me." He kissed her again.

"I have a career and a responsibility to the firm. They took a risk on me. I owe them a debt and I've made a commitment to them. I can't quit." That was it. The final easy out she could offer him before things went too far.

"Am I asking you to quit?"

"Would you ask that of me?"

Steve shook his head. "Let me make this very clear to you." Dropping his hands to her shoulders, he tugged her away from the doorjamb. "Barthelmauses don't waste anything and after spending all that time in school, throwing it away would be a waste of your knowledge and skills."

He wrapped his arms around her and held her so closely she could hear the steady beat of his heart against hers. "We believe in commitment, too. We don't make promises we don't intend to keep and when we make a promise, we keep it. You've made a commitment to your law firm. I'd be disappointed in you if you didn't keep it. Understand?''

This time Jennifer nodded.

"Good. Now I'm asking you again. Do you love me?''

Jennifer couldn't answer him. The protective shell she'd put around herself had been toughened by too many years of heartbreak to break easily.

Steve tipped her head up so she was again forced to meet his gaze. It was direct, warm and honest as always. She wanted to believe, but wanting to and doing it were two different things.

"I love you, Jennifer, and I'll never stop loving you.''

"How can you know that?'' she managed in a whisper made husky by the tangled emotions she was experiencing.

"I just do. Trust, I guess.''

"Trust?''

He smiled, the slow warm smile that always melted her. "Remember the day Stephanie was born, I asked you to trust me?''

Jennifer remembered, and remembered as well how easy it had been to trust him that day. She nodded.

"You did, and I did everything in my power to make sure your trust wasn't misplaced. I always will. Right now I'm trusting you, trusting that all I'm feeling isn't one-sided. Is it one-sided, Jennifer?'' he asked.

"I don't think what you're feeling is one-sided.'' Having taken that one tiny step and discovering it hadn't been disastrous, she dared another. "I think I do love you, Steve.''

"Come on, Jennifer," he coaxed, compelling her with his voice, his touch and his eyes. "That's not quite good enough."

Jennifer's stomach tightened and she swallowed hard. "I love you."

Steve let out a big sigh and dropped his head back. "Thank God!"

Gathering her up in his arms, he swept her into the room, lifted her off the floor and took a few jubilant turns, before toppling them both onto the bed. Before she could catch her breath, he covered her mouth, his kiss more fiery and possessive than ever before.

"You are going to marry me, aren't you?" he said, raising himself just enough to give his hands room to roam over the curves of her body.

Jennifer's hands were just as restless to explore his body. "Are you really giving me a choice for a change?"

"Not really," he admitted as he tugged her shirt from her shorts.

"Then I'm not going to marry you."

His eyes widened and his audacious grin disappeared. His hands stilled at her waist. "But, but, I love you. You love me. I want to spend the rest of my life with you."

Jennifer had a difficult time keeping from laughing. She wasn't going to make him suffer long, but she needed to get some of her own back. He'd outmaneuvered her far too many times. Ticking each point off on her fingers, she announced, "You're egotistical, domineering, bossy and just plain spoiled. I couldn't possibly marry you."

Steve stared down at her for a long moment, his expression a mixture of shock, disappointment and then resignation. Finally he said, "All right. This wasn't quite the way I'd planned to ask you to marry me, anyway." After heaving himself off the bed, he held out his hand to help her up. "Come with me. I mean would you come with me... please?"

Fearing she might have gone a little too far with her charade, Jennifer allowed him to help her up, and wordlessly they made their way back downstairs. Politely he guided her into the old-fashioned parlor at the front of the house. "If you'd care to take a seat, I have a few things to do."

Jennifer seated herself in the middle of the graceful Duncan Phyfe love seat, crossed her hands on her lap and watched Steve go about the room lighting candles in wall sconces flanking the fireplace and in the candlesticks scattered here and there. "Will you excuse me for a few minutes?"

"Certainly."

As soon as he was gone, she pressed her hand to her stomach in an attempt to still the butterflies waging a war within. She no longer feared her refusal had put him off completely. He wasn't a man who took no for an answer.

Feeling more uncomfortable and nervous with each passing moment, she crossed, then recrossed her ankles, straightened and smoothed her clothes, then worried about her hair. Spying a small round mirror on the wall over a desk at the opposite side of the room, she listened for sounds of Steve's return. Hearing nothing, she dashed across the room and did what she could to put a little order to her appearance.

The sound of his footsteps in the hallway sent her racing back to her spot on the love seat. She'd barely gotten herself back in her outwardly composed position when he entered. Under one arm was a long, narrow, but unusually thick, florist's box. Under the other was a bottle of champagne. He dangled two crystal glasses in the fingers of one hand. His other hand was tucked behind his back.

He placed the box on her lap and said very solemnly, "These are only faintly as beautiful and sweet as you."

Jennifer tried not to giggle at his formality. "Thank you." She lifted the lid and discovered a heap of pale coral long-stemmed roses—her favorite color.

"How did you know?" she asked, her eyes wide with wonder.

"I guessed and hoped since you wear that color so often."

She lifted one from its bed of ferns and breathed its delicate scent. "They're exquisite." She placed it back into the box and took a good look at the contents. "Oh my goodness! How many are there?"

"Fifty. One for each year I hope you'll spend with me."

Tears stung the corners of her eyes. Her lips trembled. "Oh Steve. . . I do love you." She sighed.

She started to tell him she hoped they would have fifty years together but he stopped her with "I'm not finished. Don't say anything else, yet."

He placed the champagne and glasses on the table next to the love seat then dropped to one knee before her. "Jennifer, I love you with all my heart. Would you do me the great honor of becoming my wife?"

Though Steve wasn't wearing a velvet cloak, or a jewel-hilted sword, and there wasn't a white charger standing nearby, he was the prince of her dreams and no fairy-tale prince could have been more handsome, dashing or eloquent. "Of course I will."

Holding out her arms, she started to embrace him, but again he stopped her. "There's a codicil to this contract, Madame Attorney." Reaching behind his back, he fumbled blindly with one hand as he said, "I give you my solemn pledge that you will always have a choice about all but one thing—my loving you." Taking her hand in his, he brought his closed hand from behind him. "As a symbol of that pledge, I give you this." He slipped a sparkling diamond solitaire ring on her finger.

Tears were streaming down her face, but Jennifer didn't care. "Now, Steve. Please hold me and kiss me," she begged, sure that if he didn't put his arms around her, she'd shatter.

He grinned at her as he opened his arms. "Now who's being bossy," he said when she fell into his arms and toppled them both to the floor.

"I said please," she murmured between kisses along his jaw.

"So you did." Rolling over with her, he kissed her long and deeply. Lifting his head after a long series of kisses, he looked at her with great tenderness.

"Jennifer... ? There's another codicil to this contract we're going to enter into."

"What's that?"

"It has to do with just one other area I'm not going to give you a choice about."

Jennifer raised an eyebrow. "Just how many more codicils are you going to tack on?"

"Just one more, I think."

"Just one more," Jennifer echoed. "Until you think of some more? I knew it was too good to be true that you promised me choices."

"This is important."

"All right. What is it?"

"If you ever give birth again, I insist you have the baby in a hospital with a regular obstetrician in attendance."

Jennifer giggled. "Oh I don't know. The doctor I had last time did an awfully good job."

"He was scared to death."

"But he had the most wonderful voice and eyes and hands."

"Maybe he could assist."

"He'd better!"

With a smile, Steve sat up, then scooped her up in his arms and carried her upstairs to his bedroom. There he worshiped her body, letting her know with his hands, lips and tongue that she was wanted, cherished—and would be for life.

*   *   *   *   *

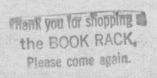

Bestselling author **NORA ROBERTS** captures all the
romance, adventure, passion and excitement of Silhouette in
a special miniseries.

THE
CALHOUN WOMEN

Four charming, beautiful and fiercely independent
sisters set out on a search for a missing family
heirloom—an emerald necklace—and each finds
something even more precious . . . passionate romance.

Look for THE CALHOUN WOMEN miniseries
starting in June.

COURTING CATHERINE
in Silhouette Romance #801 (June/$2.50)

A MAN FOR AMANDA
in Silhouette Desire #649 (July/$2.75)

FOR THE LOVE OF LILAH
in Silhouette Special Edition #685 (August/$3.25)

SUZANNA'S SURRENDER
in Silhouette Intimate Moments #397 (September/$3.25)

Available at your favorite retail outlet, or order any missed titles by sending your name,
address, zip or postal code along with a check or money order (please do not send cash)
for the price as shown above, plus 75¢ postage and handling ($1.00 in Canada) payable to
Silhouette Reader Service to:

In the U.S.	In Canada
3010 Walden Ave.	P.O. Box 609
P.O. Box 1396	Fort Erie, Ontario
Buffalo, NY 14269-1396	L2A 5X3

Please specify book title(s) with your order.
Canadian residents add applicable federal and provincial taxes.   CALWOM-2

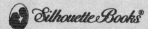 *Silhouette Books*®

Take 4 bestselling love stories FREE

Plus get a FREE surprise gift!

Special Limited-time Offer